JONATHAN AYCLIFFE

the LOST

Constable ● London

CONSTABLE

First published in Great Britain in 1996 by HarperCollins Publishers

This edition published in 2015 by Constable

A CIP catalogue record for this book
is available from the British Library.

ISBN: 978-1-47211-121-0 (paperback)
ISBN: 978-1-47211-271-2 (ebook)

Typeset in Times by TW Typesetting, Plymouth, Devon
Printed and bound in Great Britain by Clays Ltd, St Ives plc
Papers used by Constable are from well-managed forests and other
responsible sources

MIX
Paper from
responsible sources
FSC
www.fsc.org
FSC® C104740

Constable
is an imprint of
Little, Brown Book Group
Carmelite House
50 Victoria Embankment
London EC4Y 0DZ

An Hachette UK Company
www.hachette.co.uk

www.littlebrown.co.uk

Persian, Arabic and Islamic studies at the universities of Dublin, Edinburgh and Cambridge, and lectured at the universities of Fez in Morocco and Newcastle upon Tyne. The author of several ghost stories, he lives in the north of England with his wife. He also writes as Daniel Easterman, under which name he has penned several best-selling thrillers.

Also by Jonathan Aycliffe

Naomi's Room
Whispers in the Dark
The Vanishment
The Matrix
The Talisman
Shadow on The Wall
The Silence of Ghosts

This is for Beth and Nancy,
without whose constancy, love and unswerving attention
none of this would have been possible.

Acknowledgements

At the best of times, sane and professional advice make an author's life go more smoothly. *The Lost* was written under difficult conditions, and I cannot praise too highly the tender ministrations of my editorial team in London, Patricia Parkin and Mary-Rose Doherty, who ironed out problems with their customary skill and panache. A word of thanks too to Abigail Holland in New York who, coming on the scene rather later, helped get everything on track over there. Behind the scenes, Geoff Hannell kept the ball rolling with his ever-thoughtful attention. Need I say how grateful I have been for the support and love I've had all year from Beth and Nancy? Without them, I doubt if a single word would have been written.

Part I

casă feraru

Part I

1

POSTCARD FROM MICHAEL FERARU TO SOPHIE WANDLESS

Budapest

23 October

My Dearest Sophie,

I don't know what to write, or how to write it if I did. I've arrived here in a dream, like someone stumbling over a threshold he never meant to cross. All I can think about is leaving you on the platform at Victoria three nights ago. The platform here is cold and dark and wholly without cheer. I'm taking a few minutes in the station café to write a card while trying to drink something that looks like weak gravy and tastes like burned parsnips. Maybe it is burned parsnips. At least it's hot.

It suddenly all seems quite pointless, being here without you; I've already started to fantasize about the journey back, and seeing you again, and things I daren't put on a postcard. If only you'd been able to come with me. Can't you think it over again? It's still not too late, you know – you only have to make up your mind and tell old fart-face what he can do with his job.

No more space on this pygmy card. I dream of you. I'll write properly from Bucharest.

XXXXXX
Michael

2

LETTER FROM MICHAEL FERARU TO SOPHIE WANDLESS

Hotel Dîmboviţa
Bucharest

26 October

Sophie Wandless
90 Mill Road
Cambridge

Darling Sophie,

I always thought travel broadened the mind. In fact, the only thing it seems to broaden is the backside, from excessive sitting on hard seats. First, the wretched train journey from London, and now two days of sitting in hot offices, filling in forms or waiting for forms to fill in. I understand the civil service here is called 'Ceauşescu's Revenge', and I can see why. One particularly nasty cow delighted in making me wait three hours just to tell me I'd been given the wrong form in the first place, and please could I fill in another one, which turned out to be its identical twin? If my Romanian had been more fluent, I'd have given her a lesson in the democratic assertion of citizen's rights.

God, I must sound pissed off, and only here two days. Our telephone conversation two nights ago didn't exactly cheer me up. I know Derek Hignett is a prat, but you didn't have to go to dinner with him, did you? Look, it isn't that I mind you dining out with other men occasionally (actually, I do), it's just that I don't want to hear the gory details of the fabulously independent life you're leading in my absence, or how well you're coping, or the adventures you're enjoying with little turds like Hignett. He has a toupee, you know. Ask him about it sometime.

What I do wait is for you to tell me how much you miss me, that you're pining for me, that life without me is unbearable, that you have to grit your teeth every time you cross a bridge, just to stop throwing yourself into the Cam. Even if none of it's true, it's what I want to believe, and surely I have a right to be indulged. I do miss you, though – miss you and pine for you like mad.

It looks as though I'm going to spend a lot longer in Bucharest than planned. That woman at the Rom-Aid office was right after all: the bureaucracy makes Kafka look like an advert for American Express: 'How may I help you, sir?' The thing is, nobody here really wants to help, not even if you explain that you're here to lend a hand – especially if you're here to lend a hand! I'd rather fondly imagined that, the minute I told them my plan – all right, our plan! – they'd be falling over themselves to oil the wheels for me, whereas they actually seem to delight in applying as many brakes as possible. Given the chance, I think they'd happily unscrew the wheels and leave me in a basement oiling axles for the rest of my life.

My British papers aren't going down as well as I had hoped they might, and the old Romanian documents that belonged to my grandparents don't seem to carry as much weight as I thought they would. No one here has so much as heard of Vlaicu Castle, and the Feraru family doesn't seem to exist in any official files. We all seem to have got lost down a big black hole somewhere. No doubt the real files are with the Securitate, or whatever they call the secret police nowadays. It's as if I'd suddenly discovered that I'd been snatched away at birth and adopted. But no doubt we'll turn up in due course.

Even if I could clear all that up (and I haven't despaired yet), I'd still have to provide them with conclusive proof that I am Michael Feraru, that my parents were Dumitru and Rosemary Feraru, and that my father's parents were the last legal owners of Castel Vlaicu.

You may have to do some digging for me over there. I'll try to work out what they may ask for next. In the meantime, do you think you could look up my grandparents' naturalization papers? You should get them at the Public Records Office in Kew, though you may have to go through the Home Office's Nationality Division first – just ring up, and I'm sure they'll tell you what to do.

It's getting late, and I've got to be up at dawn or earlier just to get a place in a queue, so I'd better stop here. Write as soon as you get this – a letter would cheer me up no end. Especially if it were delivered by hand.

      Love and kisses,
      Michael

3

LETTER FROM SOPHIE WANDLESS TO MICHAEL FERARU

90 Mill Road
Cambridge

1 November

Dear Idiot,

Derek Hignett may be a prat, but he's not half as big a prat as you. If you must know, he took me in to town, to a singularly grotty little Indian joint on Hills Road, plied me with a truly nasty bottle of Hungarian roach-killer, and treated me to Hignett's potted history of Balti cookery. Rest easy: Hignett is not Alan Rickman, and the Agra Balti House is not Le Manoir aux Quat'Saisons.

As for you, your correspondence has about as much sparkle in it as a flat bottle of Lambrusco. I'm sure the workings of Romanian bureaucracy are almost as fascinating as the development of Balti cuisine, but I had expected something a bit more . . . shall we say, spicy? Descriptions of Bucharest, vignettes of daily life after Ceauşescu, cameos of colourful characters you've stumbled across in your local trattoria. In short, the sort of thing you're going to put in your book.

You do remember the book, don't you? It was an integral part of our – sorry, my! – big plan. Not only do you go to the romantic wilds of Transylvania to reclaim your heritage in the form of Dracula's castle, then turn said castle into 2 proper orphanage and school for the local kids; but you write an account of your adventures from beginning to end, which we then sell to a big London publisher for lots and lots of money. The money, in case, you've forgotten, is a fairly essential element in the plan, since we have to assume that, even in Ruritania, you will need liberal doses of the stuff to transform the family heap into something approaching a habitable dwelling. 'Habitable' being a prerequisite for my telling fart-face what he can do with his job.

I want to know what colour the sky out there is, how many shades of grass there are, what kinds of trees, how wide the roads are, the names of all the rivers, where to find bears and wolves and vampires . . . So, get writing. And find out if that hotel you're in has a fax.

And, yes, since you mention it, I do love you. Yes, I miss you. And, yes, I'm filled with suicidal thoughts every moment you're away. Otherwise, I'm having a perfectly splendid time with Derek Hignett and all the international cuisine Cambridge has to offer. We're doing Greek tomorrow. He knows a little taverna . . .

> One big kiss,
> Sophie

PS: The papers are being sent separately. You owe me two lots of £17.63, which comes to £35.26. If you apply direct to Kew, you can bypass the Home Office lot in Liverpool. Progress, eh?

4

Extract from the Journal of Michael Feraru

Bucharest

2 November

I suppose Sophie's right, it is time I started keeping a proper record of my visit. Now I'm here, though, I'm beginning to have doubts about whether anybody back home will ever want to read about my exploits. Most of the time I just hang around in queues or fill in forms or argue with faceless men behind ten-foot-high desks. It isn't exactly riveting.

I would never dream of telling this to Sophie, of course, but I am starting to wonder why I bothered to come. The orphanage idea's fine, as far as it goes, but I'm not convinced I'm the ideal person to run a place of that sort, and I'm not sure it's my real reason for being in Romania.

It's not that I'm unaware that aid workers aren't all that welcome here, that they're quite resented, in fact – I think I already knew that before I bought my ticket and applied for my visa.

No. I think playing at the noble aid worker in a country whose inhabitants would happily see the back of me is just an excuse. I'm in Romania because a silly, insistent little voice keeps telling me I'm a Romanian, this is my home, my roots are here, and that, if I want to discover my true identity, this is where I have to be.

None of it is true, of course, not really. I have an identity, roots, an English mother, a home in Cambridge. But the silly little voice whispers that I will not know rest until I have visited the home of my father's ancestors, stood by their graves, prayed over their bones, breathed the air they once breathed.

And is there not a part of me, however well hidden, that longs to be, just for a moment, lord of a castle in Transylvania, the heir of centuries? Like all little boys, I used to fantasize that I was different from my friends, that I'd been snatched from my true parents, and that, in truth, I was a prince or a lord. Most children entertain such thoughts; in my case, it was true.

Of course, my parents were my real parents. But they never told me anything about my father's family, except to say that they'd all escaped from Romania in 1947, after King Michael was forced to abdicate and the Popular Republic was declared. My father had been eighteen then. My grandparents' property was expropriated in 1949, when collectivization was introduced by Gheorghe Gheorghiu-Dej.

For years I thought they had left behind a dwelling much like the small town house they owned in South Kensington. It was only when I grew up that I was told the truth, that my grandfather, Iuliu, had been the last in a long line of Ferarus who, from the Middle Ages until the Communist takeover had ruled the vast feudal estate of Vlaicu in the Harghita Mountains, part of the Eastern Carpathians, in Transylvania.

My grandparents never spoke to me of Vlaicu, nor of the lives they had lived there. Instead, their anecdotes had concentrated on

11

Bucharest between the wars: King Ferdinand and the eccentric English Queen Marie, King Carol and his mistress Magda Lupescu, visits to the royal summer retreat at Sinaia, and to Bran castle for long audiences with Queen Marie; dinners at the Capşa restaurant, Gypsy bands in an open-air café on the Chausée Kiseleff, weekends at Marthe Bibescu's country house at Mogoşoaia, with its pillared loggias and its Brancovan chapel, whole fortnights with Princess Callimacki at Măneşti. I particularly remember my grandmother's mouth-watering descriptions of the confections she used to buy at Kalinzachis, a Greek *confiseur* at Sinaia, the memory of whose conserve of fresh wood raspberries still sent her into raptures.

And yet never a word about Vlaicu, never a photograph or a painting or a careless anecdote. Until I was eighteen, I had not guessed that my grandfather had been a count, or that Bucharest had been but a second home to him and my grandmother.

Now it all tugs at me, even though I know that world has gone forever. I walk through Bucharest at night, down Calea Victoriei, across the drab Piaţa Victoriei, along Şoseaua Kiseleff, or through the leafy streets of Bulevardul Dacia, with their *Jugendstil* houses and Orthodox churches like jewel boxes, and I half-close my eyes and sniff the night air and try to recapture what I never had, to recall what I have only heard. That is why I am here, why I may remain here.

5

LETTER FROM ARTHUR DREWE MA TO MICHAEL FERARU ESQ

King William's School
Old School Lane
Cambridge

1 November

My Dear Michael,

I said I'd write when you got to Bucharest, just to let you know how the old school's surviving without you. Your young woman, Sophie, gave me your address. She says you're settling in well and making a nuisance of yourself. Just like you, eh? I always used to say – sparing your blushes – 'that young Feraru will make a mark for himself one day: he's got enough cheek for a cageful of monkeys.'

No doubt it will be tough going at first, but as I once overheard one of our sixth-formers say, 'when the going gets tough, the tough get going'! Well, I'm sure that's excellent advice, especially in a tough corner of the world like Rumania (I believe they spell it 'Romania' nowadays, and I can remember when it was 'Roumania', a sort of

13

blend of the two, but I'm sure you know that already). Anyway, Michael, we are, as you know, extremely proud of you here in Cambridge. The third form are agog to hear of your adventures and to receive photographs of the young orphans you'll be taking into your care.

Mind you, I'm sure it will be some time before you get to that stage. I understand that the bureaucracy in countries that have been under the Communist yoke can be a little daunting at times, though I'm sure you'll cope, especially with your fluent Rumanian and that innate sense of order that was such a boon to us all in the years you spent with us.

Now, I did promise you some news, so I shall forthwith put you out of your misery. There is, I fear, one item of bad news to set ahead of the rest: you will remember Miss Bracewell, who taught remedial classes until a few years after your arrival here. I regret to say that she passed away almost exactly a fortnight ago, after a prolonged struggle against breast cancer. I attended the funeral, of course, along with Marjorie Neville and Kevin Barnes.

More happily, you will be pleased to hear that Miss Rutherford has become engaged to be married. Her fiancé is a respectable young man from Newmarket, a junior manager in a firm of computer specialists. She intends to stay on after the wedding, though I do fear we may lose her once the first little one comes along.

As I mentioned in passing, third form are eager to do a project based on your experiences in Rumania, and Mr Bryce has asked me to pass on a request for anything that may help them: maps, photographs, travel posters – you know the sort of thing. He did say you weren't to send any babies: I suppose this is an example of Brycean humour, though I have heard there is something of a trade in children from that region. It is such a tragedy, and I cannot say too strongly how much we all admire the initiative you have taken, even if it has taken from us one of our most competent and best-loved teachers.

Well, Michael, I hear Jean's dulcet tones summoning me to the evening repast. Having said *bon voyage*, I now wish you, on behalf of everyone at King William's, *a bon séjour* and every success in your charitable endeavours.

All the best,
Arthur Drewe

15

LETTER FROM MICHAEL FERARU TO
SOPHIE WANDLESS

Hotel Dîmboviţa
Bucharest

6 November

Dear Numskull,

I've just had the most awful letter from the Arch Druid. He says you gave him my address. I'll never forgive you. This is worse than Derek Hignett. You could have given him a false address and put my failure to reply down to the rank inefficiency of foreigners: he'd believe that like a shot.

I've been asked to send things to help the third-formers with a project on Michael Feraru's Big Adventure. It's tempting to send a few slices of raw *slănină* and a couple of 'I ♥ Romania' stickers.

I'm not so sure I love Romania myself. It's early days yet, and I know I shouldn't be judgmental, but I find it quite hard here at times. People are just so rude, they go ahead of you in queues, they play loud music and to hell with everybody else, and they try all sorts of scams if they think you're a foreigner (which, when it comes down to brass tacks, I am). Worst of all are the petty bureaucrats, whose only purpose in life seems to be making other people's lives hell.

Mind you, I have met some very friendly types, and they tell me these are just things they all have to put up with. Some put it down to years of Communism, some say it's the national character, and one suggested it was the heritage of the Ottoman Empire. Oh, well, I'll survive.

The search for the missing Feraru millions continues apace. I've found the most wonderful assistant (and, yes, she is female, and, no, I'm not in the least bit tempted), a young lawyer called Liliana Popescu. Liliana graduated just after the revolution, and as a result failed to walk into the state job that had been waiting for her under Ceauşescu. She scrapes together a living by translating legal texts from English (which she speaks well), mainly for local import-export companies.

Liliana tells me I've been going about things completely the wrong way. Apparently, the last thing to tell a Romanian bureaucrat is that you're here to open an orphanage. They're (understandably) rather sensitive about the whole issue, after the terrible publicity the country got when the old regime orphanages were opened up and photographs splashed all over the world's newspapers. It all got worse when aid money and aid workers started flooding in, and worse again when most of the money got siphoned off into the pockets of ex-Securitate and the like.

So, it seems that the right approach is to say nothing about orphans, orphanages, or aid, and to behave like a proper capitalist entrepreneur from the decadent West. Liliana says I should tell them I want the castle back (a) because it's mine and (b) because I want to open an hotel. Hotels mean tourists and lots of hard currency coming this way.

A business means the possibility of bribes. And a grateful foreigner could mean jobs for relatives.

It looks as though I'm on the right track at last – expect good news in my next letter. In the meantime, Liliana's getting on to the legal side of things – filing my claim to Castel Vlaicu, digging up details about the family, establishing my identity and my right to the inheritance. She thinks there may be more than the castle involved, that I may be entitled to other properties, including a town house here in Bucharest.

And, since you're probably asking yourself the same question, the answer is 'yes': Liliana is doing all this free of charge, in the expectation that, if it all pans out, I'll come into money (or property that can be turned into ready cash) and be in a position to pay her a proper fee. It's what American lawyers do, apparently, when they agree to represent somebody in a lawsuit the client can't afford – if you don't win, you don't pay. Seems fair enough to me.

Look, I know I don't say very much, but I do love you a lot, and I'm missing you dreadfully. I've got three photos of you on my bedside table, like a little shrine, and I worship at it daily. There's the one of you at Freddy's wedding, looking terribly smart and pissed as a newt. That was when your hair was long, of course, so I've got two others with it the way it is now (which, as you know, I prefer). But I suppose you've dyed it black or red or something now, and when you come here you'll tell me I've been worshipping a false goddess.

Liliana asked me to describe you yesterday, and I said you were a sort of cross between Meg Ryan and Michelle Pfeiffer. She said she hadn't heard of either. That's the sort of place this is. I tried her out for a while, and the only well-known blonde-haired women she could come up with were Dolly Patton and Ivana Trump. I told her that wasn't quite the image I had in mind.

You don't need to worry, she's no rival for my affections. There *are* no rivals for my affections. As I said, I'm not tempted. Liliana's no Romanian beauty. She's not ugly, I don't mean that, in fact she's quite nice looking, if you go for that type, which I don't. She's small and dark-haired, but not the sultry temptress type, if you see what I mean.

XXXXX
Michael

7

Extract from the Journal of Michael Feraru

Bucharest

---

7 November

The longer I remain here, the deeper the illusion becomes. Time is stripped away, like a coarse bark, and I find myself walking streets my father walked, and looking up in a moment between afternoon and evening, in a half-darkness, and seeing briefly with his eyes. A lighted window, perhaps, and a woman's shadow half concealed, or a partly-opened doorway from which the sounds of muffled festivities escape.

I walk a little further, and more of the bark is stripped back, and I am my grandfather at the fall of night. A Russian tango, *Dwe Gitare*, sweeps from behind a painted screen, the scent of apple blossoms fills the air, a gate swings open in the black and gold railings that mark the boundary of a great villa, and I seem to hear the rush of a carriage being driven between the lime trees of Chausée Kiseleff, the horses at full gallop, black Orloffs, as rare as precious icons.

Illusion piles on illusion at times, until I am quite buried beneath them, and the squalor and ugliness of modern Romania seem things quite forgotten, as though the drab years had not been, and everything had remained unchanged. For minutes at a time now, I become my father and my grandfather, as though they have crept deep inside me and come to life again. And I wonder how long it will be before the others come to inhabit me, my grandfather's father, and his, and his, in that long, snaking line that stretches back, how far I do not know and cannot guess.

Our name is not Feraru. That was almost the first of Liliana's discoveries. With her help, I have made more progress in a few days than in all the time before this. Feraru was a name taken by my grandfather on the union of Transylvania with the rest of Romania following the signature of the Treaty of Trianon in 1920. Before that, our name was Vlăhuţa, plain Vlăhuţa.

Well, perhaps not so plain. We were an ancient Vlach family, one of thousands that had entered Transylvania from neighbouring Wallachia in the twelfth and thirteenth centuries. In 1010, an ancestor of mine, Mircea Vlăhuţa was raised to the nobility and given Castel Vlaicu and the surrounding lards as his fiefdom.

Somehow, we survived the fluctuations of Austrian, Ottoman, and Magyar rule, and the daily intrigues of life in such a hotly disputed territory. We continued to exist and, if we did not flourish, at least we managed somehow to fend off generation after generation of greedy Magyar neighbours ready to make use of the smallest pretext to take our lands and castle, our serfs and livestock, and whatever wealth we had hoarded away.

That's as much as I know at the moment about the history of my family in Transylvania. Liliana's just finished giving me a short lecture on the history of Moldavia, which is on the other side of the

Carpathians, to the east of Transylvania. Moldavia was more or less pure Romanian, even if it took centuries to gain real independence. One of the leading *boyar* families was a branch of the Vlăhuţas, known as Feraru. The Ferarus had risen from almost nothing by offering loyal service to the Ottoman sultans, who had ruled Moldavia since the early sixteenth century.

To begin with, the Turks were happy enough to make use of local nobility like the Ferarus to run things for them. But that all changed in the eighteenth century, when they began to send governors out from Constantinople. The Ottoman Empire had already started on its long downhill slide, and the system of appointing *hospodars* to Moldavia and Wallachia shows that. The post went to the highest bidder, who would then run his new territory like a personal holding, screwing as much as possible out of the local population either to hold on to his position or to take back with him when his term ended.

The candidates all belonged to Greek Christian families from Constantinople's Phanar quarter. These Phanariots, as they were known, were a tightly-connected little mafia whose only loyalty was to themselves.

There were a few exceptions, of course, *hospodars* who took their role seriously and stayed on beyond the two or three years necessary to amass a private fortune. Liliana waxed quite lyrical about one shining example of enlightenment despotism, a certain Constantin Mavrocordato, a reforming *hospodar* who seems to have been a cross between the emperor Joseph II and Frederick the Great.

The Mavrocordatos had no reservations about marrying into the ranks of the local nobility, and like several other *boyar* families, the Ferarus took advantage of this opportunity in the hope they might hang on to some of their houses and most of their serfs. For a while, the Moldavian branch of my family became the Feraru-Mavrocordatos,

22

and while Phanariot rule lasted, they did very well out of their Greek connection.

When Constantin Mavrocordato died in 1769 much of his family returned to Constantinople. Some of the Ferarus went with them, the rest stayed on. Phanariot rule continued for several decades longer, and finally ended in the early part of the last century. By the 1830s, the *boyars* had regained most of their ancient rights and privileges.

Moldavia and Wallachia were united in 1861 to form a new kingdom of Romania, and there were the Feraru-Mavrocordatos, ripe and ready to enjoy the good life as courtiers under the newly established Romanian royal family. Unfortunately, intermarriage with the effete Mavrocordatos doesn't seem to have done them much good, and by the 1870s it was obvious that the entire line was in imminent danger of dying out.

In the meantime, there were the old Transylvanian Vlăhuţas, stuck up in the mountains in Castel Vlaicu, surrounded by Hungarians and Saxons ready to dispossess them the second they got the chance. It wasn't until 1920 that Transylvania got its chance to join Moldavia and Wallachia as a province of Romania, but well before that the Vlăhuţas had taken pre-emptive action. One – of them I'm really not quite sure which one, but I think it might have been my great-great-grandfather, a man called Vasile – married one of the last of his Moldavian cousins, a young girl by the name of Alina. Their descendants kept the Feraru-Mavrocordato name for a generation or two, but when Transylvania joined the rest of the country, the second part was dropped.

It's a most disconcerting feeling, to find and lose yourself in one and the same moment. Something has been added to me, and something else taken away. I feel cast adrift, unable to decide whether it is safer to paddle back the way I came, or to strike out boldly for the horizon. But perhaps safety is not what counts after all. I am thirty-one years old, I have been a schoolboy, and a student, and a teacher, nothing more. Now, I am to be whatever I choose to make myself. Or I am to become whatever it is in my blood to become.

I do not yet know why my grandfather, Count Iuliu, decided to change his name. The simplest explanation is that the old Phanariot associations of Mavrocordato no longer seemed appropriate in a kingdom founded on the myth of Romanian solidarity. For the moment, that is what I mean to believe. But it does not explain why, for all those years, he said nothing to me of our true name and our proper history, or why, for even longer, my father preserved his own silence regarding all these things. But I have never been a refugee, I have never had to make a totally fresh start in life, as they did. How can I know? How can I understand?

8

CLIPPING FROM THE *CAMBRIDGE ADVERTISER*,
7 NOVEMBER

LOCAL TEACHER TAKES ON EX-COMMUNIST BUREAUCRACY TO BUILD HOSPICE FOR AIDS KIDS

Michael Feraru (31), former teacher of English at King William's School, is the latest to join the small army of gallant British volunteers working to rebuild ex-Communist Romania after years of suffering under the notorious dictator Nicolae Ceauşescu. Appalled by television scenes of conditions in Romania's Victorian-style orphanages, and by tales of babies and youngsters condemned to an early death by treatment with contaminated blood, Michael gave up his job at King William's, where he had worked for eight years, and set off for Bucharest.

Michael's former headmaster, Arthur Drewe MA (63), has told the *Advertiser* in an exclusive interview, of his former teacher's struggles with obstructive Romanian bureaucrats, men and women trained by the infamous Securitate secret police and still running the country, even after Ceauşescu's downfall. Mr Drewe spoke recently with Sophie Wandless (26), Michael's love-lorn girlfriend, who has stayed in Cambridge, but is in constant touch with her intrepid partner.

'Sophie tells me that Michael has had some hair raising run-ins with the secret police out there, but he's handling the situation well, with true British grit and determination. Apparently he's hoping to find a disused hotel or something of the sort to turn into an orphanage for about one hundred children. Once he has it up and running, he'll be asking for volunteer help from agencies in this country.'

Your reporter, Julie Rahman, asked Mr Drewe if there was anything readers could do to help Michael in his efforts.

'We're setting up a support scheme at King William's, and your readers could send gifts to Michael through us. Money, of course, and things like bedding, bandages, old clothes – I'm sure Michael will need all he can get. I've written to him recently, and I'm sure I'll have a fuller list for you to print in your next issue.'

Readers with items for Michael's orphanage should send them to the Romania Relief Project at King William's School, Old School Lane, Cambridge. We'll be keeping in touch, and we hope to have a report from Michael himself in a coming issue.

9

Extract from the Journal of Michael Feraru

Bucharest

---

8 November

Today, Liliana found a faded photograph of Castel Vlaicu. I've just pasted it in the page facing this. Later, it may be published in my book, perhaps used as the jacket illustration.

It shows a dark place, high among mountains, surrounded by what appear to be winter trees. There are traces of snow on the mountains behind, and on the branches of the higher trees. A narrow path winds up to the castle from a valley far below. It is not, of course, a castle in the sturdy English sense at all, being more a confection of high towers topped by narrow steeples, slanting roofs furnished with cupolas and lanterns, and corbelled overhangs that seem about to topple at any moment into the depths below.

The photograph is of poor quality, but I can just about make out differences between one section of the castle and another: it seems to have been added to at various times, sometimes in wood and sometimes in stone. One part boasts a high stone tower with a steep, crenellated parapet. There are few windows, and no lights in any of them. Even allowing for the age of the photograph and the state of the weather when it was taken, it all makes a rather dismal scene, and one I suddenly feel reluctant to visit. It does not seem a happy place, and I begin to wonder if my plan to turn it into an orphanage can be such a good one after all.

Liliana says she is making some progress on the property title front. She has received official consent to file an application in my name, laying claim to Castel Vlaicu and its dependencies. Any properties in Bucharest can be handled separately, she says; but she would prefer to get moving on the castle first, mainly because it seems to have been my family's principal residence. Apparently, getting your actual 'home' back is do-able – especially if you want to turn it into an hotel and line a few pockets in the process – whereas asking for half of Bucharest into the bargain could screw things up.

The full process of application will pass through innumerable stages, so the sooner we get the whole thing under way, the better. All the same, I am beginning to wonder just what it is I've set in motion.

Most of Liliana's time is taken up with investigations into the history of the Vlăhuţa family, since the whole transaction will stand or fall on a demonstration of my right of ownership on the basis of centuries-long occupation until 1947.

'One thing I really don't understand,' she said to me today while we were having lunch, 'is how on earth your family ever held on to Castel Vlaicu in the first place.'

'Why not? Back in England we have families that go back to William the Conqueror and beyond. It's certainly not unusual to hold on to an estate for generations.'

She shook her head.

'That's not what I mean. Romania isn't England, or France, or even Italy. No, don't laugh – it's just that our history is much more complicated. You can't believe how many wars, how many invasions, how many squabbles between this empire and that. Transylvania has always been a very mixed region – different races, different religions, different destinies. Now, the Romanians are in control, but that is very recent, within living memory only. In the Middle Ages, it was not so. Only three peoples – three "nations" – held power: Hungarians, Székelys, and Saxons. For Romanians, like Gypsies, there was nothing except hard work and hunger. Many would leave for Moldavia, to have a better life. But for those who stayed, there was much suffering and little freedom.'

'If that was the case,' I interrupted, 'surely the Vlăhuţas would never have owned land or become nobles.'

She gave a slight shake of her head. A lock of hair fell across her forehead, and she brushed it back with an unconscious motion of her hand.

'I'm not sure, Michael. To become noble was very hard for Romanians, but not impossible. A few families rose to positions of influence. They had money or military skills, or their women were beautiful. Some even became all-powerful, like John Hunyadi, who was made *voivode* and whose younger son became king of Hungary.

'No, that is not what surprises me. What I do not understand is how your family held on to their position for so many years. I am not expert in the history of Transylvania, but I know it is extremely rare, perhaps without parallel.'

I smiled and wagged an admonitory finger.

'Perhaps no one dared to steal our lands. Perhaps my ancestors were vampires, whom no one dared to challenge.'

To my surprise, I saw her face go pale. I let my hand fall back to the table.

'You should not speak about such things,' she said. 'Not even in jest.'

My hand lay unmoving, between us. I looked at her eyes, at her dark skin. There was no hint of mockery in her face.

Something else happened this evening as I was walking back to my hotel. I had been at the Central Library on the Piaţa Revoluţiei, and was on Ştirbei Vodă. A group of Laetzi Gypsies had gathered on the corner, where Ştirbei Vodă joins Strada Buzeşti, at the north-west corner of the Grădina Cişmigiu. There were about six of them, three men and three women, the latter dressed in wide, brightly coloured skirts. The men were begging, rather unsuccessfully, it seemed, while the women offered to tell fortunes for passers-by.

Seeing me approach, one of the women guessed right away that I was a Westerner and a likely target for their attention. She turned to me, smiling, a pack of Tarot cards displayed in one hand. I saw her turn, and thought nothing of it, having passed *tziganes* like these almost daily in my walks about the city. But as I made to pass her – for I knew that to stop would be to invite the tedium of barely comprehensible platitudes about life and love, and the inevitable request for *lei* – an aspect of her features or her movements arrested me.

There was in her face something alert, a look of cunning or shrewdness that puzzled me, so strongly did it contrast with the usual sullen and defeated look of a Romanian gypsy. I paused and peered at her more closely: it was impossible to say what age she was with any hope of precision, not even if she was young or old. Her eyes above all carried such a piercing and intelligent intensity that I almost looked away.

But even as I looked, I saw her expression change and her quick movements slow and halt. She stared me full in the face, eye to eye, as though seeking there confirmation of some terrible secret, some hidden knowledge that could not be spoken aloud. And then I saw her eyes widen and a look of utter horror fill them and spread until her entire face was a mask of fear, fear that changed in a moment to anger. She stepped forward, hissing at me, mouthing words in her own tongue, words that meant nothing to me. I stepped back, as though reeling from physical blows. And as I did so, I, saw her friends turn and stare at me, their own eyes opening, and that same frightened, hate-filled expression on their faces.

I turned on my heels and ran, leaving behind me the sound of the woman's voice, harsh now, bright with menace, or so it seemed to me. I did not stop until I had set them far behind, almost out of sight, and out of hearing. But even now, sitting in my room, I fancy I can still hear that woman's voice, shrill and violent, ringing in my ears. And if I close my eyes, I can see her face, and the fear in her dark eyes.

I said nothing about the incident to Liliana. She might have laughed, arid dispelled my unease. But it was too much to risk. She might not have laughed at all.

10

LETTER FROM MRS ROSEMARY FERARU TO MICHAEL FERARU (RECEIVED 9 NOVEMBER)

The Queen Marie Guest House
York Villas
Harrogate
Yorkshire

4 November

Dear Mikey,

You must be wondering what's become of me. There you are, practically on the other side of the world, and not a word from your mother. The truth is, dear, that I've been quite rushed off my feet. We've had a stream of conference delegates staying since September, and it's all just starting to tail off now. Everyone seems to have been to Harrogate this year: the International Potato Seminar, the West Yorkshire Rose Growers Annual Meeting, the Georgian Houseowners Association – even the Annual Conference of Pet Bereavement Counsellors!

Brenda went down with this ghastly flu at the beginning of October, and she's only just back in action, so I've been doing twice as much as usual. Touch wood, I haven't come down with it yet myself, but people are dropping like flies – you're much better off out of it, for I'm sure the air in that dreadful school is positively saturated with the virus by now.

I did get your letter last week, darling, and I was so pleased to hear that things are going smoothly at last. That awful woman in the Ministry of whatever-it-was sounds absolutely unspeakable. We have some types like that here now, of course. A little revolution wouldn't do us much harm, I'm sure, provided, of course, it was a sensible sort of revolution led by somebody like Mrs Thatcher, who'd soon sort them out. I know you don't altogether approve of her, dear, but you must admit she took this country by the scruff of the neck and made foreigners treat us with a little respect again. If she'd been dictator of Romania instead of that awful Mr Ceaușescu, she'd have got them in shape.

Of course, the dear Romanians are to be admired for having got rid of Ceaușescu and his wife, but are you really sure that Iliescu and co. are still Communists? Surely not. I mean, there has been such liberalization since the revolution, and you would hardly be there if the people in charge were really still Communists, would you? I'm sure it's all some sort of misunderstanding: obviously, in the old days absolutely everybody had to belong to the Party if they wanted to get on, so I wouldn't be surprised if all the really capable people had been apparatchiks. You'll have to ask around, but I'm sure you'll find things aren't as bad as they seem to be.

You did ask about your grandfather and this castle you're planning to turn into the orphanage. To be perfectly frank, dear, I know next to nothing about your father's family. None of them ever spoke much about the old days, and, of course, when I was first married I was a perfectly silly young thing, and not much interested in family history.

33

Of course, I did know that your grandparents had been aristocracy, and I won't deny that I was quite thrilled at the time to have married into what we thought of as old European stock. I expect, now that everything over there has changed, you must be entitled to call yourself Count Feraru or Duke Feraru or something of the kind. And I may very well be a countess, though I expect it wouldn't do for the proprietor of a guest house in Harrogate to go around putting on airs of that kind. All the same, it's nice to know, isn't it? I'll probably get myself a tiara and wear it shopping at Safeway.

I have been able to find an old photograph album in one of your father's trunks: I'll send it out to you by registered post, if you think it might be of some help. There were a few letters as well – I'll pop them in the packet with the album, so you can have them all together.

I suppose it must have been as a result of my digging about after these family relics that I had the most vivid dream a few nights ago. Do you know, dear, I haven't dreamed of your father in years, but that night he was as true as life, and a round the age he was when we first met. He was terribly pale, though, not like himself at all, and he kept trying to tell me something, as if he wanted to warn me about some danger, but the words wouldn't come, however hard he tried, just occasional fragments that made no sense. He whispered your name a few times, so perhaps his warning was to do with you. Ordinarily, as you know, I pay no heed to such things, but this dream has stayed with me ever since. I can't seem to shake it off. Maybe I am coming down with this wretched flu after all.

Anyway, Mikey, I just think you should be careful. You are in a foreign country after all, and you can never be too sure what may happen. It's a good thing you speak the language so well. Otherwise you'd be quite at their mercy. But one can never be too careful where foreigners are concerned, even if you are almost one yourself!

That's just my little joke, Mikey, I know you don't approve of my opinion of other races, but I do wish you'd pay heed to some of what I say – it's not all nonsense, you know. The Romanians were Communists for a long time, after all, and as you've already discovered to your cost, they still have a long way to go before they shake off the effects of that terrible time. So do be careful, and write to me often. I expect to have a quiet spell between now and Christmas, and with Brenda on her feet again I'll have more time on my hands. By the way, Brenda and the others send their love, as do your Auntie Nancy and Uncle Frank.

Not to mention that Sophie of yours, who loves you most dreadfully, you know. I know you think I'm a bit of an interfering old busybody, but I am your mother and I do care about your happiness. I rang Sophie last night, just for a little chat, you know, to see how she's getting along and find out if she had any messages for you. She was in good spirits as usual – such a cheery girl, and so polite. But, then, you hardly need me to tell you that. All the same, she was most awfully upset that she's scarcely had a peep out of you all this time. One little postcard and a three-page letter.

Now, darling, I know you hate it when I poke my nose into your affairs, but Sophie is such a dear girl, by far the nicest of the girlfriends you've had, and so much more our sort of person than that Lizzie Hindmarsh you were going with before, and whom you know I never liked. And, of course, Sophie does come from such a nice family, it would be such a shame if there was any sort of *upset*.

Well, darling, I won't say another word, but I do think you should put pen to paper straight away and get a letter off to that sweet girl. In fact, I don't see why she couldn't have gone out there with you, but that's none of my business, and I won't mention it again. If you'd married her in the first place, I'm sure you'd have taken her with you, but it's all living together and 'trial marriages' nowadays. All the same, if you don't want to lose her, you'd better pull your socks up.

I asked Betty's café to put together a food parcel for you a few weeks ago – a couple of cakes, one or two packets of tea and coffee, and some chocolate. More at Christmas, of course. I did want to send some Yorkshire Fat Rascals, which you love so much, but they told me they wouldn't stay fresh in the post. If you want some, you'll just have to come home soon. Do you need any books sent out? Just let me know the titles, and I'll make up another parcel. Food parcels. Just like the war!

All my love,
Mother

11

EDITED TRANSCRIPT OF TAPE-RECORDED NOTES MADE BY MICHAEL FERARU

'Testing, testing . . . one, two, three, four, five six . . . Mary had a little lamb, its fleece was white as snow; every day it shagged her silly, ee-ay-ee-ay-oh. OK, this seems to be working. Hard to believe, really . . . it's a Russian job, a bit of crap really, but all I could afford. The tapes don't look as if they're up to much either . . . Right, here goes . . . It's . . . God, I've forgotten the bloody date. Just a tick . . .

[PAUSE.]

'Right, it's the ninth of November, and I'm sitting here in my bedroom feeling like a twerp. It's ironic, actually, I'm surrounded by tins of cake and – what the hell are these? – giant fucking bars of chocolate, and I'm in a country where you can't get decent food for love or money, in fact the average *alimentara*'s got less on its shelves at any one time than my precious mother can pack into a single parcel. Let's have another dekko . . . Jesus Christ, this parcel's probably worth about fifty times their entire stock, I could live for several months from the proceeds if I sold this stuff on the black market.

'Just look at it: ginger and walnut cake, Old Peculier fruit cake – spelt with an "e" – sloe gin fruit cake . . . what the hell's this? – panforte di Siena? From Harrogate? Venetian festival cake, likewise from Harrogate, fresh cream liqueur truffles, fresh cream champagne truffles, mint serpents, butter shortbread, chocolate biber biscuits . . . And what about the "one or two packets" of tea? China Gui Hua, China Emperor Keemun, Mountains of the Moon broken pekoe, Yunnan flowery orange pekoe, Special Estate Tippy Assam . . . it goes on and on like a catalogue of vanished empires.

'The coffee's just as bad. Let's see . . . French Roast, Vienna Roast, Italian Continental, Yemeni Mocha "Heights of Araby" Ismaili, Monsoon Malabar Mysore, Jamaica Blue Mountain Peaberry, Puerto Rico Yauco Selecto Peaberry, Cuban Sierra del Escambray, Ethiopian Mocha Harrar Longberry, Sumatra Mandheling, she's even got something in here called Colombian Medellin Excelso. Mother hasn't got herself into a cocaine ring, has she? I can just see the headlines: "Police Smash Medellín Drugs Cartel in Harrogate Guest House. Widow Under Arrest."

'Actually, I'm surprised the bloody parcel made it through customs at all – not because it might have had drugs, but because of all this wonderful food. Things are still pretty corrupt here, I'm told the situation's much worse than it was under the Ceaușescus. I can . . .

[CLICK. HISS.]

'Bugger, the bloody thing started rewinding on me. Hope it hasn't wiped much. I want to keep some stuff on tape that I'd rather not put in the journal. Private stuff. I can always review it later and tone it down for official use if it seems OK, otherwise, I can keep it on tape as a reminder.

'I've been spending some evenings with Liliana and her old classmates. They're mainly a bunch of former law students from the university, and some hangers-on from different faculties, mostly literature and history, and they all get together in one another's flats to drink *ţuica a*nd raw *rachiu*, and talk about everything from sex to politics.

'They're a funny lot on the whole, and I'm not really sure what to make of them. Most of the time, they just sit about getting professionally pissed, which seems to be the thing to do in Romania. But then they seem to have a Jekyll and Hyde switch, and go all intense on you, and start philosophizing and arguing politics, and before you know it, what started out as a drinking binge has turned into a fucking postgraduate seminar, and then they're all . . . what is it? Yes, I know, they're all modelling themselves on fifties and sixties French bohemians, you know, it's as if the girls all want to be Juliette Greco, and the boys are budding Sartres, and all that's missing are the Gitânes. Maybe mother can start a French cigarette smuggling ring. She'd make a bomb.

'They . . . Actually, they don't seem to have much of an opinion of me. It's partly, I suppose, my being a foreigner. I mean, there's a real resentment of outsiders coming here to show the Romanians how to run their own country and live their lives. I made the mistake of trying to reassure them, and all that happened was I ended up laying it on a bit too thick about my Romanian origins, and then the whole bloody thing backfired when they found out my grandfather had been a count, and next thing Liliana just blurts out I'm here to reclaim the ancient family estate . . . She made a great joke of it, but most of them weren't laughing.

'What was that one of them said last night? "I despise the Communists, but I despise your sort even more." He was really quite angry. "The *boyars* kept this country back for centuries. Now, idiots like you are trying to bring back King Michael and start all that nonsense over again. We didn't throw Ceauşescu out just so we could put another puffed-up dictator in his place." He was a ratty little bloke,

39

mind you – bad skin, rotten teeth, and dirty hair. Bloody Bohemian Rhapsody . . .

'I said I wouldn't want Michael back if he grew two heads, and I tried to parade my own left-wing credentials – I'd always voted Labour, I couldn't stand Margaret Thatcher, I belonged to various Third-World charities, but it didn't cut any ice. I'm not sure half of them even knew who Margaret Thatcher was! All that mattered was that my grandparents had cleared off for greener pastures while theirs had been_ forced to stay where they were and go through fifty-odd years of unimaginable hardship.

'It doesn't even help if you say you support the revolution. "What revolution?" – that's what they normally say if you bring it up. "Nothing's really changed. If anything, conditions are worse for ordinary people than they were under Ceauşescu. All of us here would have had jobs back then, now we're on the scrap heap because the economy can't support us." And on and on like that . . .

'I remember one girl a couple of nights ago. "There was no revolution," she said. Just like that, flat and to the point. She was younger than me, a year or two anyway, but even so, I felt like a child sitting there beside her, she seemed to have packed years into months and become old in a short time. "Believe me, the whole thing was a set-up job from beginning to end. Iliescu, Brucan and Roman – they set it all up with General Militaru, years before the riots started. Get back issues of *România Libera* out of the library, there are dozens of articles all saying the same thing. There was a conspiracy, and now the conspirators are in charge. Nothing has changed. Nothing will change."

'I've stopped arguing with them. I find myself alienated by them, they seem so without hope, without use for their liberty. Nothing matches up, but they can't see it. They say I can find articles about the

40

conspiracy in the library, freely available to anyone who asks: what sort of conspiracy is that? I'm beginning to think they don't deserve democracy, that, at heart, all they're good for is a dictatorship – leftist or rightist, it doesn't really matter. They despise my grandfather, but I know what he'd have made of them. At least he was cultured, cosmopolitan, polished. All that's gone now . . .

'Bugger this thing. They don't want a revolution, they just want things to work. I don't know . . . Hang on, I've got to change the tape . . .

[PAUSE.]

'Right, that's done. I think I'll ask mother to send out a Sony or something. It'd be a lot more use to me than all these biber biscuits.

[PAUSE.]

'I've changed my name to Mihai, which is Romanian for Michael, my real name, if you like, and given time I may drop Feraru as well, and return to Vlăhuţa. I'd call myself Vlăhuţa Mihai, like the Romanians do, but not yet: one step at a time, eh?

'At Liliana's suggestion, I've moved to an apartment near the university. It's a lot cheaper than staying in an hotel, and it helps me feel like a resident and not the tourist I've been. Now, when I walk the streets at night, I've got a proper address to return to. I feel more Romanian every day, less English . . . it's almost as if . . . as if something's reawakening in me, something I didn't even know was there.

'I don't know if it's just coincidence or the result of a more sinister process, but the night before mother's letter arrived I had a dream about father, too. He was pale and tired-looking, and he seemed to be standing in a clearing among dark woods, staring at me. There was an expression in his eyes that reminded me of the Gypsy woman. He stared at me for a long time, and at times he'd open his mouth and

41

try to speak, but I heard no words, however hard I listened. Just . . . just wind . . . in the trees, rustling the leaves and moaning among the branches, a cold wind . . . above a dark clearing, and . . . and my father . . . staring all the time . . . and his speechless . . . open mouth forming words I couldn't hear. It was dark when I woke up, and for a long time I could hear the sound of a cold wind among trees.'

12

LETTER FROM SOPHIE WANDLESS TO MICHAEL FERARU (MIHAI VLĂHUŢA)

90 Mill Road
Cambridge

7 November

Dear Nincompoop,

You really are a misery-guts. First, days without a word from you, then a horrid letter all about how down you're feeling, how you're starting to hate your fellow Romanians, and how rotten life is in Bucharest. Well, Michael – sorry, Mihai! – let me tell you, it could be a hell of a lot worse. You could have Derek Hignett pestering you for what he's started to call 'dates', and you could have a horrid nine-to-five job in an insurance office in Huntingdon.

Oh, dear – I mustn't be too hard on you, I suppose. You're obviously suffering from culture shock, just as I predicted, and you haven't got me there to make it better. I will try to get out for a week around Christmas, as I promised, and then you can grumble all you like before I take you off to bed and take your mind off whatever it is that's bothering you.

43

All this Vlăhuţa business sounds terribly exciting. Do you think your ancestors really were vampires, terrorizing the neighbourhood and passing some deadly longing on in their genes? Have you checked your teeth in the mirror lately? Or do you find an inexplicable reluctance to look in mirrors at all these days? Thoroughly creepy, isn't it?

Actually, talking of 'creepy' – Arthur Drewe was in touch again yesterday. I wish you'd do something to get him off my back. I may be your official girlfriend, but I'm not your bloody unpaid secretary. He means well, I suppose, but he is a dratted nuisance. It's not just stickers for the third form now, I'm afraid. He's started up some sort of 'Aid for Romania' scheme at the school, and I think he's planning to get enough money together so he can inflict a bunch of his sixth-formers on you at the holiday.

I've told the old buzzard the orphanage scheme's far too undeveloped to make it worth anyone's while going out to Romania at present, but he chooses to treat me as an illogical female and tells me that it's precisely because things are so 'far behind' that help is urgently needed and – thanks to the pupils of King William's – on the way. He's got the local rag running some sort of weekly progress report, which is why he rings me so often, in the hope of a snippet of news or a piece of idle gossip.

Speaking of 'official girlfriends', I certainly hope you're telling me the truth about this Liliana person, because if I find out you've been bedding the little bugger, Arthur Drewe will just have to start a 'Medical Aid for Michael Feraru' scheme. Lawyers aren't all that interesting, as I should know. You may remember my telling you about the ghastly Ronald Pemberton-Clewes and his penchant for going over his case notes in bed. He once tried to do it with me wearing his beastly wig. I went into convulsions, and he had to sit up all night holding my hand and talking about torts or something.

Actually, it isn't really funny, I feel terribly vulnerable without you. I miss you dreadfully, and I worry about you. I know you're being faithful, but sometimes I wake up in the middle of the night and imagine things. I can't help it.

In fact, darling, I had the queerest dream last night, and I still feel quite jumpy when I think of it, so I thought I'd tell you about it. It concerns you anyway, or I think it does. Really, Mike, it was the most vivid thing, as if I was there, not dreaming at all. I was in a forest of some sort, or, at least, I was surrounded by tall trees, and there was a high wind, and the most fearful clattering of leaves and branches. There must have been light from somewhere, moonlight possibly, for I could see an old man standing near me, not above six yards away, staring at me with his eye; wide open and his mouth opening and shutting.

He was in his late sixties or early seventies, and when I close my eyes now and imagine his face, he reminds me of you. Even though not a sound escaped his lips, they were moving almost constantly, and several times I was sure he mouthed your name – very distinctly, as if desperate I understood, and with a look on his face as if he was terrified out of his wits.

It left me quite shaken. God, I wish you'd been there last night, even if it was just to tell me I was being silly. I haven't admitted how much I miss you, how hard it is here without you.

But I wasn't being silly. That dream wasn't like any dream I've ever had before. It's been with me all day, it's with me even as I write, I can't shake it off. For some reason, it's left me anxious about you. I telephoned your hotel this evening, but they said you'd checked out, that you'd taken an apartment in town, they wouldn't tell me where, and they didn't have a telephone number. The clerk said they would be forwarding mail to you, so I'll just have to depend on that.

45

Please write as soon as possible, even better, phone if you can.
I need your new address. And I need to know you're safe.

All the love in the world,
Sophie

13

EXTRACT FROM THE JOURNAL OF
MICHAEL FERARU (MIHAI VLĂHUȚA)

Bucharest

10 November

The photograph album arrived today, and with it a bundle of letters. The letters are old, very old some of them, and difficult to read, being written in a formal Romanian hand and a style that baffles me. My written Romanian was never up to much anyway. I'll ask Liliana if she can make sense of them, when she has time.

She's quite unlike any of her contemporaries, different to any Romanian I have met so far. Where they appear touched to the soul by Ceaușescu and his vile regime, creatures born of an evil moment in an evil place, she seems wholly free of that taint, as though her spirit cannot be darkened by any shadow that may fall across it. She is wholly lacking in the moroseness that so mars her friends, and instead talks with optimism about the future and stoic resignation about the past.

Her parents brought her up in a small village in northern Moldavia, a region where Ceauşescu's collective farming schemes remained a dead letter, and where she was cushioned from the worst excesses of the regime. In general, peasants suffered more under the *conducătór* than townspeople, but in places where his long arm did not fully reach, there could be compensations for the hardships of daily life. Food could be grown in private and either hoarded or sold on the black market, and if you were fortunate enough to live in a spot far removed from the concrete sprawl and belching chimneys of the dictator's utopian nightmare, life could be bearable.

That isn't to say that Liliana's family were not desperately poor, or that existence in their backwoods community was not at most times harsh and drab. But her grandparents remembered better times and a different way of life, and Liliana herself had been brought up to know that no nightmare, not even the seemingly interminable one of life under Communism, would last for ever. She still believes it, and when their moaning makes her angry, she mocks her friends and tells them what they can do with their negativism.

If I'm to be honest, I have to admit that I'm becoming drawn to her, that she is exerting an increasingly powerful effect on me and my feelings. I wake in the middle of the night, in that horrid, honest hour before dawn, when there is nothing but candour between us and our inmost thoughts, and I find myself thinking, not of Sophie, but of Liliana.

I find her attractive in the most unexpected way. I always thought I preferred blonde-haired women with light skins, but Liliana's dark: dark-haired, dark-skinned, dark eyes – so dark, in fact, she seems to smoulder. She's small, and she looks so frail she could almost have stepped out of one of those sanatoriums I'm told they have up in the Carpathians. But it isn't just her physical attractiveness that gets to me, it's the way she seems so much at ease with herself. She makes me believe in her, makes me want to get closer to her in order to be part of whatever she is. And that makes me want to undress her, to make love to her, to spend every possible moment in her company.

I won't let it go any further, of course. I'm alone in a strange city, a foreign country, and it's only natural I should be disorientated for a while, in need of comfort, desperate for reassurance, for someone to focus my thoughts and feelings on. That will all change when Sophie comes to visit. If Sophie didn't exist, or if she left me, things would be quite different, that goes without saying. But I do love her, and she loves me, so there's no question of letting things get complicated.

I am growing certain – more certain with each day that passes – that something awaits me here in Romania, something that has been waiting for a very long time. It's a feeling I find harder and harder to shake off, a conviction, almost a knowledge. We all come by degrees to some measure of our destiny, and in time, if we live long enough, to its fullness. Until now, I had no sense of destiny, no illusion of personal worth. I still don't know what sort of shape my life may take, but I know now it will be moulded here, for better or worse.

14

TRANSLATION OF A LETTER FROM
LILIANA POPESCU TO NICU CARACOSTEA

București
Stradă Alba Iulia Nr. 17
Blocul 7
Scară C
Etajul III
Apart. 45

10 November

Cea mai dragă Nicu,

You remember the mad Englishman I told you about in my last letter? The one whose grandparents were aristos who buggered off after the war and left everybody else to get on with it? Well, it looks as though he's buying your little scheme, just like you said he would. He's already paying me to fix things up for him here, and if I play it right there could be decent money out of it in a month or two.

He's the real thing, of course, which makes it all workable. He calls himself Mihai now, and I don't suppose it'll be long before he starts styling himself *Count* Mihai. Still, the Americans will just love it if he does.

All I have to do is convince the right people he's entitled to have his castle back, and it all starts happening. He has people lined up at home, ready to send out hard currency as soon as he has this thing up and running. I've persuaded him to clam up about this stupid orphanage idea, and to tell the authorities he's planning to open an hotel. By the time I've worked on him, he'll think going into the hotel business was his own idea and his reason for coming to Romania in the first place. And then I introduce him to a close friend who just happens to have a diploma in hotel management . . . Not to mention a lawyer who can smooth his path with the authorities and fix the best contracts with suppliers.

Actually, I think he's starting to get a bit sweet on me. Don't be jealous, darling – he isn't remotely my type. He's not bad looking, if you go for the Woody Allen intellectual sort. I don't mean he's weedy, but he does look very intensely at you, and I think he could be moody. Of course, if you take the modern clothes and the specs away, I suppose he could pass for one of his ancestors: the Englishman's just a veneer, he's all Romanian underneath. And I needn't tell *you* what Romanian men can be like.

All the same. I think I should play him along a little. If I can get his heart involved, he'll forget his head completely. I've no intention of sleeping with him or anything, so you needn't fret. And don't, for God's sake, come to Bucharest. The key to this whole thing is timing, which means keeping you out of sight until it's all set.

Radu says 'thanks' for the bottles. All the same, you shouldn't encourage him: he's drinking far too much these days, and if he goes on like this he'll end up back in that awful hospital. I'm terribly fond of Radu, so go easy with what you send him. And lay off it yourself, if you know what's good for you.

It's almost midnight. I'd better stop here: I've got to get up early to start digging about in the Land Registry for details of my friend's family mansion in Bucharest. It was probably knocked down years ago, but there's no harm in looking.

Amor vesnic
Lili

15

LETTER FROM MRS ROSEMARY FERARU TO MICHAEL FERARU (MIHAI VLĂHUŢA)

The Queen Marie Guest House
York Villas
Harrogate
Yorkshire

10 November

Darling,

I hope you've received the parcel I sent out, with the photographs and everything, and I do hope those terrible customs officials don't hold up your food parcel either. There are some perishable items in there (I have written on the outside, and I got young Peter Ionescu to put it in Romanian as well – he's a charming boy, and he's been seeing rather a lot of Brenda recently, though I can't say I would positively encourage it, she's rather beneath him, if you don't mind my saying so, though I suppose you do. But I like to think there are still some standards), so any sort of delay would be most inconvenient. You must write back to me the minute the parcel arrives and let me know what condition everything arrived in, and how long it took. It's not far to Christmas now, and I want you to have an especially large hamper this year.

Now, Mikey, you remember asking me to look for photographs, which I did, and have sent on, as per request. But while I was hunting up the really old ones, I came across lots of lovely snaps from the old days, when your grandfather and grandmother were still alive, and your dear father, of course. I don't want to put them all in the post, because I would be too upset if they were to get lost, the post office is so careless these days, and you can't trust anyone like you used to, anyway, I've put some in an envelope and written 'PHOTOGRAPHS DO NOT BEND' on the front, not that they'll pay the slightest heed, they never do, do they?

I'm sure you've forgotten our day out in York on your tenth birthday. I'd always thought the snaps we took that day had been thrown out by accident, but there they were in a biscuit tin in the attic, as right as rain. There's a lovely one of you and dad in the Castle Museum, in that little cobbled street with the funny Victorian shops, and one of you holding up the fishing-rod your father bought you, looking ever so proud and ready to catch your first fish. In fact, there's another photograph here of you that your father took the following week, when he took you trout fishing in the Derwent, up by Bickley Forest. I wish you'd gone on with the fishing, it was a thing your father loved, off on your bikes early on a Saturday. I know you never caught very much, but that wasn't the point, was it? I think you'd have got to know your father better if you'd gone more often. Of course, in Romania it would have been bear-hunting or some such in the mountains, only we don't have a lot of bears in Yorkshire. But he never complained. He was a lovely man, your father, he never complained about anything.

Your grandfather came with us that day, the day of your birthday, which is something he didn't do very often, being fonder of his own company than ours, as a rule. He quite enjoyed himself, kept saying the old parts of York reminded him of places he'd known back home. Do you find that at all, that Romania reminds you of York? I don't expect so, they've all changed, nowhere's the same as it was. It's a thing we elderly have to endure, you'll find the same yourself one day, you'll not recognize the places you thought were familiar.

An odd thing was that your grandfather wouldn't set foot in the Minster. He made such a fuss, and in the end we went in without him, you, your dad, and I, while your grandmother stayed outside to keep him company. To this day I can't think what the reason was, but he just said there was an atmosphere about the place he didn't like. I always thought it queer, though when I spoke to your father about it afterwards, he wouldn't give me a straight answer, and I thought there was something he knew but wasn't telling me. A few times that happened between us, but I thought nothing of it, your father was a lovely man, if he had any secrets, they can only have been small ones. Your grandfather was more of a mystery, you could see there were things he wouldn't tell just anyone, not even in the family. But I suppose him being a count and responsible for important affairs would have made him like that.

Well, dear, I feel quite tearful, thinking about the old days, and the good times we used to have, and your poor father, and that terrible dream I had of him, which I can't seem to get out of my mind. I feel he's closer to me now than ever, and sometimes as though he's there, just looking over my shoulder while I write this . . .

I'd better get this to the post box before the van comes. Write soon. And let me know about that parcel. Brenda sends her best wishes.

Your loving mother
XXX

55

16

EXTRACT FROM THE HEADMASTER'S JOURNAL, KING WILLIAM'S SCHOOL

10 November

The very worst time of year. Over half the term gone, and a distinct feeling in the pit of the stomach that not a quarter of the allotted tasks have been done, or that they have not been done to satisfaction. There are moments when one feels it might not be such a bad thing after all to be out there in the public sector. It would, of course, be merely to exchange one set of problems for another – but at times one does almost long for fresh preoccupations.

The board of governors is proving quite demanding this year, especially that new woman in the dreadful pink hat, Mrs Blair-Fawcett. The current bunch aren't in the least interested in the school's academic achievement per se, only in so far as it might relate to profit margins, and accountability, and staff pension funds. All important enough in their way, I daresay, but not what the school is all *about*. They barely listened to my report on how many senior boys had won scholarships and exhibitions, nor were they thrilled to hear of young Allsop's organ scholarship at Trinity (and it such a magnificent achievement for a young man with a hearing impediment).

I am concerned about the Wren Hall roof, though. Maws, the surveyor, sent in his report this week, and it makes grim reading. There's no question of putting the fees up again, not for a year at least, and that would not even begin to cover the cost of a new roof in any case. Still, the governors did come up with one good idea, once their initial shock wore off. We're to hold a gala concert for Founder's Day this year, maybe even turn it into an annual event. King's choir school might agree to let us have a few choristers, which would bring in decent numbers. And the Hall is a Grade One listed building, a sterling example of Wren at his peak – much finer, in my opinion, than his earlier chapel at Pembroke. I'll ring Dan Freeman at English Heritage tomorrow, and see if he has any suggestions.

On the subject of fundraising, we're doing very well getting money together for the Rumanian appeal. It's been the bright spot in an otherwise bleak year so far. All the boys who plan to fly out to Bucharest over the Christmas hols have been able to persuade their parents to cough up, which means that all the money collected so far – £2,784.07, according to young Matthews – will go straight to the orphanage, or at least to the purchase of essential commodities for it. There is some talk now of hiring a minibus to take the volunteers, instead of flying them out, and using it to ship some supplies. The whole project has given focus to the school this term, and I'm only sorry the roof is likely to interfere next year.

I was a trifle disturbed by something that happened this evening after prep. Two of the fourth-formers, McGill and Andrews, came to see me in my study. They are both pleasant boys, if a trifle ebullient at times. Neither has the makings of a scholar, though they perform well enough on the rugby field, and Andrews shows promise as a rower. They are not imaginative boys, indeed, I should have said they were rather on the dull side.

When I saw them, they seemed unusually ill at ease. I thought at first they had a guilty secret to divulge, though I thought it strange they should come to me directly, instead of to their House Master. On reflection, I do see that I was the right person for them to bring their trouble to: Mr Marsden is a rather stern man, and a hidebound sceptic. That is not to say that I believe all the boys told me; but I am disinclined to dismiss it out of hand, or to make fun of them for telling me.

It seems that McGill and Andrews had gone together to Bodley Stairs last night before dorm. I suspect they had gone there for a sly smoke, but I saw no reason to press the matter. Of course, I may have a quiet word with Boyd, the sports master, or Rawlins, who is in charge of fourth-form rowing this year. Smoking and rowing do not mix, and the foolish boy could spoil his chances of a place on the school eight if he keeps it up.

They told me they had settled down for a chat – comparing notes before today's Latin test, according to McGill – and that the stairs were deserted. Everybody else was in School House preparing for dorm. It seems they had been there for five or six minutes when Andrews heard something moving above them on the staircase. McGill says he could hear nothing at first, then a sort of rustling. The stairs are not particularly well-lit at that time of night, and they could see nothing. Andrews thought one of the masters might have gone up to fetch something from a classroom. But the more he listened, the less likely that seemed. It was a furtive sound, not the sort a man would make if he thought he was alone in an empty building where he had every right to be.

What happened next is the unpleasant part. It frightened the boys badly, and I must admit it did little for my own nerves to hear them speak of it. Andrews was, it appears, about to call out, when he heard another sound, much closer and more intimate than before: a sound of muffled whispering, as though someone unseen were actually present on that stretch of staircase, speaking in hushed tones.

McGill heard it too. He says that the voice was an unpleasant one, the like of which he fervently hopes never to hear again. After a minute or so, both boys' nerve broke, and they ran off. Andrews says he is certain that, had they remained and had the voice continued, it would have quickly grown unbearable, and that something more dreadful would have happened. He cannot say exactly what this 'something' might have been, nor can he explain why he is so inwardly sure of it. Nonetheless, I believe he is telling nothing but the unadorned truth.

The boys have told no one other than myself of the incident, for fear of ridicule. But they have been badly frightened, and they dread a repetition of the episode. Bodley Stairs have indeed had a reputation for being haunted as far back as I can remember. But none of the stories associated with earlier hauntings seem to match up with what Andrews and McGill have related to me. Their story has none of the characteristics of a deliberate hoax – I know a frightened schoolboy when I see one.

There is, of course, no ghost – I know that as well as Ronald Marsden – but someone may all the same be playing silly games. Such things are hardly unusual in a school like this. Or there may be a more unpleasant explanation. One thinks, these days, all too readily of drugs. One or two senior boys have been expelled for dabbling in illicit substances. I shall say nothing to other members of staff, however, until I am more sure of my ground. I intend to pay a visit to Bodley Stairs myself tonight.

17

LETTER FROM MICHAEL FERARU (MIHAI VLĂHUȚA) TO SOPHIE WANDLESS

Bucureşti
Calea Dorobanţilor 118
Blocul 11
Apart. 4

11 November

Darling Sophie,

Good news at last. Liliana has tracked down our old house here in Bucharest. When I say 'our', I mean the family, of course – the Vlăhuţas. It's strange, but until now I have never really felt any particular sense of family, any connection to my ancestry stronger than a vague notion that they made me a little different. Tracking down the house has made all that seem somehow real, as though a mist had begun to take on concrete shape and substance. Liliana showed me some old papers today, and looking at them, seeing my family's name on them, it felt as though I had come home after a long absence.

Amazingly, Casă Feraru survived the Communist takeover and the depredations of Ceauşescu. I haven't set eyes on it yet, but Liliana tells me it's quite a grand building with a *Jugendstil* facade set on a more antique structure, in the Bulevardul Dacia, near where it crosses the Calea Victoriei. It appears that the house was sequestered by the government under Gheorghiu-Dej, back in 1950, and turned, first, into a club for Young Communists, then into a home for the insane, and latterly an annexe for the university's department of psychiatry.

I've arranged a visit for tomorrow – unofficially, of course. My presence as the house's putative owner would, apparently, cause some embarrassment, so Liliana has had a quiet word with a friend of hers, a lecturer in psychology, and he's fixed it so I can go over with him as a 'guest lecturer' or whatever.

I practise Romanian hard every day now, reading and writing as much as talking. It comes surprisingly easy, as though I were remembering, not learning. You'd be impressed. Maybe I'll take it up seriously when I return, take another degree or something. I could get my old job back and teach the boys Romanian!

That reminds me – will you please ask old Drewe to go easy on the publicity for his fundraising scheme? I know he means well, and I'm grateful for all he's doing, but he could put a spanner in the works if he keeps it up. As I said in my last letter, I'm having to tell people here that I'm planning to open an hotel in the castle. They can understand that and go along with it, whereas the moment you mention the word 'orphanage' their eyes glaze over and you know, you absolutely know you won't get any further. And, to be honest, I'm not sure this country doesn't need good hotels more than it does orphanages. Western aid is all very well, but the Romanians have to learn how to stand on their own feet sooner or later. From what I've been told, I may be doing more harm than good opening up another orphanage. It creates resentment, and it doesn't necessarily address the underlying problems.

I'm sorry, this must all seem very boring from where you're sitting. The fact is, being here has had a profound effect on me. I can feel myself changing, almost daily, as though something has been wakened in me that I never even guessed was there. You ought to think very carefully about coming out here: it won't be as simple as you think, and conditions here are still a bit Third-World. I'm dying to see you, of course, but I just want you to be sure what you could be getting yourself into.

But don't, for God's sake, imagine this has anything to do with Liliana or anyone else. You did sound rather, well, jealous, in your last letter, but I can assure you you're worrying over nothing. I've never been one for sleeping around, and I don't expect to start now. My relationship with Liliana is strictly lawyer–client, and I intend keeping it that way. I'll preserve my virtue here in Bucharest, if you promise to keep Derek Hignett on a short rein.

No, when I say you should think about coming out here, I'm thinking about you. Conditions really are quite rough at times, and everything's still uncertain. Obviously, this will all change once the property business is sorted out. In the meantime, you do need to be sure what you're getting yourself into. Think about it.

Be sure to give my love to everyone.

Write soon.

Love as always,
Mihai

18

EXTRACT FROM A LETTER FROM MRS ROSEMARY
FERARU TO MICHAEL FERARU (MIHAI VLĂHUȚA)
(RECEIVED 12 NOVEMBER)

. . . Mikey, I have to tell you that I had that dream again, or if not exactly that dream, one very like it, and even more disturbing. It was not your father whom I saw this time, but another man, one very like your dad when he was older, and dressed in odd old-fashioned clothes, foreign-looking clothes, and wearing the most enormous hat I've ever seen. There was something dreadfully emphatic and unpleasant about his face – even though it was so like your dear father's face – and he did stare so hard, right at me, as though he was looking inside me. It makes me shudder to think of it.

When I woke up, I was in a cold sweat, and I was sure you were in some sort of danger over there. You'll think me odd, but far just a moment after I woke, I was sure there was someone in the room with me. I don't think it was your father, dear. And I'm sure I heard someone whispering.

Will you write to me, Mikey, please, just to reassure me, let me know you're safe. You're so far away, and it's cold and dark here . . .

19

EXTRACT FROM THE JOURNAL OF
MICHAEL FERARU (MIHAI VLĂHUȚA)

Bucharest
_____

12 November

I have just read my mother's letter. It was waiting for me when I got back from my visit to Casă Feraru, innocuous in its Woolworths envelope, its Harrogate postmark, its stamps bearing the Queen's head. My mother is given to dreams and portents. I think little enough of them, but today I am not so sure; today I doubt everything, most of all myself. Home and sanity have never seemed so far away.

We went to the house this afternoon. Liliana came with me in order to introduce me to her friend, Doctor Vladimirescu. He's a man of about my age – short, amusing, unassuming, and a fluent English speaker, entirely self-taught. Within moments of our meeting, I discovered that he is also a fervent admirer of P. G. Wodehouse, whose stories he regards as faithful portrayals of everyday English life.

It is his great ambition to visit England at least once before he dies – during Ceaușescu's rule he was forbidden to leave Romania, now he cannot afford to do so. I was, therefore, a sort of consolation prize, and was treated accordingly, with the sort of deference one might reserve for a visiting head of state. I did not, I think, quite come up to his expectations of English eccentricity, though I fancy he may by the day's end have seen in me a potential subject for close professional scrutiny.

We arrived just as most of the staff were finishing for the day. Vladimirescu and Liliana had planned it like that, in order to gain time to see round the house without an audience. My arrival excited no interest. I was introduced to no one, and merely tried my best to stand in the background looking Romanian. If Vladimirescu or Liliana spoke to me, they did so in Romanian, and called me 'Mihai'. I kept my answers curt.

Vladimirescu busied himself with little tasks, while Liliana and I hung about, as though we had as much right as anyone else to be there. The building emptied bit by bit, and a slow silence descended in room after room; suddenly we found ourselves alone, the sole occupants of my grandfather's house. I wanted to cry out, to fill the silence with my sudden presence, with the knowledge that I had returned, as though, in some way, the house or someone in it was waiting. Listening.

Room by room, we set out to explore, stripping away with our naked eyes all the accretions that had overgrown the original fabric. I can't say how far the others could see past faded paint and crumbling plaster, but to me it was as if the recent past had never been, and I could see clearly, as if through time. Every cornice, every moulding, every pane of glass spoke, not of madness or grief or decay, but of the elegance that had been here once.

For all the changes in use to which the house had been subjected, the basic structure had been little tampered with. A door had been blocked up here, a false wall inserted there; but in general, the rooms had been left much as they had been before the fall from grace. Fireplaces had been left intact – unused, grimy, chipped in places, but on the whole untouched. The Art Nouveau decoration had been painted over or left to accumulate dirt, but its lines had lost little of their former beauty.

By a combination of common sense and intuition, I labelled each room to my satisfaction. This, I told myself, had been the dining room, and that the morning room, and those three rooms, now separated by plasterboard, had once been the ballroom. In one room – the library it had certainly been, for the original shelving was still there – I experienced a sense almost of déjà-vu, for on the gallery, veiled in dust, was a little shield bearing my family's coat of arms. From that moment, the sense of homecoming grew stronger.

There was, in reality, little of interest for either Vladimirescu or Liliana in the house. The doctor had seen much of it before, and to him it was merely another place of work. He's very charming and all that, but I honestly don't think he has had many opportunities to develop any sort of aesthetic sensibility. I'm sure the attractions of *Jugendstil* design were lost on him, and he could hardly have been expected to have any feeling for the house itself. Liliana was more curious, but she's really quite a pragmatic type, and before very long I could see she was getting bored.

In the end, I just left them to have some coffee and a chat about mutual friends, and set off alone to explore the upper floors. It was quiet there, for the house was set back from the unending sound of traffic on the boulevard below. All sounds seemed to fade as I climbed – first Liliana's voice, raised in laughter at something Vladimirescu had told her, then the swish of passing cars, and finally the metallic banging of the central heating boiler as it cooled down.

At first I felt elated – by my aloneness, by my closeness to a past that has come to matter more to me than the present, by the curious sense of belonging that had caught hold of me. I went from room to room, like a man who is searching for something, although he has forgotten what it is he seeks.

The rooms on the first floor had been badly mauled. At one time, they had been turned into cramped sleeping quarters, each divided into units by wooden partitions. They were now chiefly used for storage, but there still hung over them an air of palpable misery, as though their former inhabitants might at any moment return and again take possession of their rusting beds and their dim, crazed lives. A smell of carbolic hung in the air, faintly, like a mirage.

I climbed higher, and the silence grew around me, urging me to soften my tread and hold my breath, as though any sound I made might awaken more than memories.

On the next floor, almost nothing had been touched. Here, the few fragments that remained of my birthright had been cast aside to moulder and rust. Just before the house was taken from them, my grandparents had been able to salvage a few possessions – some books, some paintings, a handful of jewellery, a few objets d'art. Afterwards, Party bosses had filled their own houses and secret coffers with our furniture and anything else they could lay their hands on. What little remained had been unceremoniously dumped upstairs, in what had been the servants' quarters, among the beds and chairs and tables they had left behind.

I wandered from room to room, as if through a bric-a-brac shop or a poorly kept museum. My family's past had suddenly become tangible to me; again and again I stretched out my hand to touch a piece of it, and with each contact, I felt myself lifted up and restored as its rightful owner. Old sheets, mouldy with damp and shrouded in dust, were draped everywhere. I swept them aside, uncovering ornaments and toys, boxes and leather cases, broken mirrors and discarded books.

In a drawer in a tall chest, I found a china doll, curled up as though sleeping, and almost free from dust. It was a charming thing, at least one hundred years old, a fair-haired child dressed in a long frock. The hair – real hair, it seemed – had rotted a little, and the frock was stained, but the trace and hands were untouched by either time or accident, and I knew it would take only minor work to make the whole thing like new. I lifted it out carefully, thinking it might make an unusual present for Liliana.

I think now that I may have disturbed something in the act of removing the doll. What it was I do not know, nor have I any desire to find out. I was conscious at first of nothing more than a vague feeling of uneasiness. The elation I had felt on entering the upper floor of the house evaporated, leaving me instead with a prickling sensation across my skull, and an ill-defined sense of dread. Putting such feelings down to nothing more than the intense silence and eeriness of the abandoned, shadow-riddled rooms, I went on with my explorations.

Still clutching the doll, I chose to go out through a door at the rear of the room. I thought it would take me back to the corridor from which I had come, but instead the door opened onto unexpected darkness. I scrabbled nervously on the wall to my right until I found a light switch. It lay buried beneath a dense mat of cobwebs, and as I touched it I felt long legs scuttle away.

A weak bulb fluttered into life, revealing a short corridor that had been boarded up at one end. At the other extremity, a few yards to my left, stood a door that looked as though it had not been opened in many years. The sense of vague dread returned, stronger than before, and with it came an indistinct feeling that I was being watched. Had

I not been a confirmed sceptic, I think I might very well have turned and bolted then.

The door was not locked. The handle stuck at first, then gave way abruptly, and with a push the door swung inwards. I fumbled on the wall, but there was no switch. What light entered the room came only from the bulb behind me, a thin light that might at any moment stutter and fail.

The room seemed at first to be quite empty. There had been a window, but at some time it had been boarded over with thick, strips of wood, nailed closely together. A carpet of dust and what appeared to be mouse droppings lay over bare floorboards. No one had set foot in here in a great many years, perhaps not since my grandfather's time. The walls were covered with faded paper which, on closer inspection, seemed to have a pattern of pink roses set against green trellis.

As my eyes adjusted to the light in the room, I saw that it was not entirely empty after all. Something indistinct stood in one corner. I approached it slowly, all the time straining to see more clearly. It was low, no more than three feet in height, and about four feet long, with a higher, rounded section at one end. It was only as I came within a couple of feet that I realized what it was: a child's cot, made from wood.

Inside, a pillow and blankets had been left to rot. Something had made its nest there, and at one end I noticed what I took to be the small bones of a rat or a large mouse. A smell of decay rose from the inside. I turned my face away. Since entering the room, my feeling of disquiet had intensified.

It was as I turned that I heard the first sound, low and indistinct, somewhere to my right. I looked round, thinking that Liliana or Vladimirescu had grown tired of waiting and followed me upstairs, but there was no one there. And again the sound came, quite unmistakable now – a man's voice, whispering. The voice was pitched so that I could not quite make out individual words, only the bald impression of words, hanging in the cold air.

Hard as I listened, I could make no sense of what was said, but the tone made me shiver. There was something hateful about the voice, something that made me want to turn and run, while holding me fascinated and unable to move a muscle. The voice continued, rising in volume, yet still muffled, and behind it I could hear the beginnings of another sound, a shuffling noise, as though someone were crossing a bare wooden floor. I listened with mounting horror, for I knew the room was empty, that no one living was beside me or near me, but that I was not alone.

Out of the corner of my eye, I caught sight of something moving. With an effort, I turned my head. The cot had started to rock gently back and forwards. A baby's cry shot through the whispers, and a protracted whimpering began. At that moment, the light in the corridor went out and the door of the room slammed shut behind me.

20

EXTRACT FROM THE HEADMASTER'S JOURNAL, KING WILLIAM'S SCHOOL

12 November

There is something in the school. Something evil. I cannot begin to guess what it may be, but of its existence and its malevolence I am no longer in any doubt.

I heard it on Bodley Stairs tonight. Hard as I try, I cannot rid myself of that abominable chattering.

21

Transcript of a telephone conversation between Liliana Popescu and Nicu Caracostea

13 November

LP: '*Alo, Nicu?* Thank God you're in, I . . .'

NC: 'Lili? This is a surprise. I thought you'd forgotten all about me. You haven't rung in weeks. I had your letter this morning. What's wrong? You sound worried.'

LP: 'It's my Englishman, Nicu . . . He . . . I don't know, things aren't working out as I planned. There may be a problem.'

NC: 'He wants to screw you, is that it?'

LP: 'No, that isn't it. He was . . . Look, you know I was looking for his family house here in Bucharest?'

NC: 'Sure. You thought it had been knocked down.'

LP: 'Well, it hadn't – though I'm not sure it shouldn't have been.'

NC: 'I thought you were keen to get it as a fallback in case the deal with the castle falls through.'

LP: 'I was, but . . . something happened. We went there yesterday.

He went upstairs to wander round. It's a big house, on Bulevardul Dacia. I used to pass it on my way to the Piaţa Românа metro. It's that big house with the monkey-puzzle trees in front.'

NC: 'Yes, I know the one you mean.'

LP: 'Everything seemed OK at first. I was downstairs chatting with Petru Vladimirescu.'

NC: 'Who?'

LP: 'Petru? You remember – he's . . . Look, that's not important. heard Mihai come down, but . . .'

NC: 'Mihai?'

LP: 'For God's sake, Nicu, don't you listen to anything I tell you? Mihai's the Englishman. His real name's Michael, but since he's Romanian . . . Look, why don't you just listen for once? After a while, when he hadn't come back, I went out to look for him. He was in one of the offices, shaking. Just sitting there, staring at the wall, and shaking like a bastard.'

NC: 'He's on something?'

LP: 'That's what I thought, but it wasn't drugs, believe me.'

NC: 'How can you be so sure? Not everybody gets the same withdrawal symptoms.'

LP: 'Listen, Nicu – he hadn't even smoked cannabis before he met me. He hadn't taken anything – he'd had a fright, a bad one. It was something he heard upstairs. Or saw. It spooked him, that's for sure. He was in a bad state when I got to him.'

NC: 'Still sounds more like a bad trip than anything else.'

LP: 'He said something about a cot. And somebody whispering. It didn't make sense, except . . .'

NC: 'Except what?'

LP: 'Nicu, Listen carefully, and don't interrupt. This is serious. When I was going through the papers to prove Mihai's claim to the

73

house, I came across some files – old Securitate files. They shouldn't have been there at all, but I think they were transferred after the revolution and just left behind. You know what it was like. Most of it was the usual junk – transcripts of phone conversations back as far as the fifties, reports from informants, security assessments for anyone living or working at that address.

'But one of the files looked a bit different to the rest. It was labelled "Disturbances at Psychiatric Clinic No. 7, Bdul. Dacia, Bucureşti". There was a blue Securitate Office stamp on the front. Central Office.'

NC: 'You shouldn't fuck about with things like that, Lili. Not even now.'

LP: 'I told you not to interrupt me, Nicu. This is important. I thought I'd better take a look inside: there could have been information in there that would help me make a better case. What it turned out to be was a bunch of stuff that had been filed by the police and the Securitate. Old stuff, most of it, from about 1950. All sorts of things, Nicu: postmortem findings, psychiatric reports – there was even a sort of treatise by a Uniate priest.

'Anyway, all this stuff was connected with the house in some way. Now, listen, this is really strange: it all started while the house was being used as a youth club. Some young people committed suicide. Half a dozen in two years. And the club got to be really unpopular, till nobody was turning up any longer.

'Later on, when they started using the house as an asylum, some of the patients said they'd seen things and heard things. Of course, nobody really thought anything of it at first – you'd expect loonies to hear things, wouldn't you?'

NC: 'Speak for yourself.'

LP: 'Only, after a while, some of the staff admitted they'd been

74

seeing and hearing things too. Then a nurse was found dead on the top floor, and a year after that a doctor took an overdose and died in the same room. All the details are in the file.'

NC: 'Jesus, Lili – what's wrong with you? A few people do away with themselves, some loonies start hearing voices, and all o a sudden you believe in ghosts.'

LP: 'Listen, for God's sake, will you? You haven't seen the file, you haven't read those reports. I didn't take it seriously myself until I found Mihai in that state. He'd never read any of those papers – he didn't even know they existed – but what he said tied in.'

NC: 'What ties in? Another nutter comes along and thinks he hears God in an attic. Big deal. The streets are full of them. Just your bad luck to get picked up by one.'

LP: 'He doesn't think it's God. Just whispers, words he can't make out. And that's not the only thing. I told you he found a cot up there. In one of the reports, a very early one, it says that when workmen went to the Vlăhuţa mansion to do repair work, they found a cot on the top floor. There was something in it, Nicu – a child's body. It had been there for years.'

22

EXTRACT FROM THE HEADMASTER'S JOURNAL, KING WILLIAM'S SCHOOL

13 November

I heard the sound; again last night, at about the same time, and again a couple of hours later. They have left Bodley Stairs and are in the Headmaster's House. I think Jean cannot hear them. She has said nothing to me, although I can tell that my own behaviour is making her concerned. The voices are quite loathsome. I don't think I can stand to hear them again. I have understood a little of what they say. Dear God, can such a thing be possible? At times there is the note of menace I observed on the first night, then a tone of supplication or enticement, as though they were threatening and beckoning at the same time. How horrible if one were to be seduced by such a thing.

23

EXTRACT FROM THE JOURNAL OF MICHAEL FERARU (MIHAI VLĂHUȚA)

Bucharest

27 November

Every day now, the weather grows a little worse. There has been snow here and in the Carpathians, and I'm told there's more to come. If we don't leave soon, it may be impossible to get to Castel Vlaicu before the thaw. I spend my days reading and waiting. Since my experience at the house, walking the streets holds no charm for me. I have not gone back, and I have told Liliana I have given up any thought of reclaiming the property. She has not protested. I think she understands.

Yesterday, I opened the photograph album sent by my mother. I had put it to one side, along with the letters, and almost forgotten about it. It's a large album, bound in green morocco leather, tooled, with the Vlăhuța coat of arms embossed in gold on the front. I have no memory of it as a child. Indeed, I remember once asking my father if he had any old photos of himself and being told that all the family albums had vanished with the house. He must have kept this well hidden, whether in the trunk where it was eventually found, or somewhere else prior to its transfer, I cannot guess. I've written to my mother, asking if she knows what went on, and whether there is anything else of interest in the trunks.

I've started to take both her dreams and mine more seriously. My own experience in Casă Feraru makes me unwilling to dismiss it all as an example of her overwrought imagination or my oversensitivity. It's as if my arrival here has triggered events in a world just touching this one. But to what purpose? And what has my father been trying to warn me of?

The photographs are fairly run-of-the-mill stuff, dating back to somewhere round the end of the last century. Women in long dresses and big hats, men in military uniform and bristling moustaches. I recognized my grandparents at varying, ages, mainly together, and my grandfather on his own or with small groups. Several photographs had been taken in a studio owned by a Greek named Spyridon Papadiantis. Others had been taken at a variety of locations, most unrecognizable, a few suggestive of country houses or royal palaces.

My recent reading in Romanian history has been a little help in deciphering some of the photographs. There are faces I can recognize or guess at confidently on the basis of illustrations I have seen elsewhere. Ion Bratianu, manifestly ageing, prime minister for the fifth time, in a top hat next to my grandfather; Queen Marie, looking vaguely spiritual and terribly confused, with my father on her knee; Marie, her husband Ferdinand, the American singer Loie Fuller, Barbo Stirbey, and my father, all dressed for a game of *oina*; an older Marie, with a rather sad expression on her face, seated alongside my grandparents and my father outside her retreat at Sinaia; the future King Carol with his mistress Magda Lupescu standing on the steps of Casă Feraru.

There are older photographs too, from the period shortly after Romanian independence. Sometimes, there are dates, sometimes the place name has been recorded, and in several instances there are written details of the event being celebrated – an engagement, a wedding, a christening, an outing for *Sîmbătă Mortilor*, 'the Saturday of the Dead'. It is a whole world encapsulated, a world as dead now as Troy or Carthage. The dead look out from the pages of the album, trapped in their little rectangles of glossy card, as though struggling to see into another world. But when I close the book, they are returned to darkness.

With a little effort, I have been able to put names and faces to several of the less important people who appear regularly in the album. My father and my grandparents, of course. Then, by a process of comparison and elimination, my great-grandparents on both sides, various aunts, uncles, cousins, and the like, many of whom undoubtedly correspond to names I still remember from childhood. I make wild guesses as to who is who, using as clues the anecdotes recounted so vividly by my grandmother. One young man with prominent ears and uneven teeth must surely be my father's uncle Nichifor, known to the entire family as 'Big Ears'; and the woman with the oversized bust and heavy eyebrows will no doubt prove to be my great-aunt Marthe, who is said to have shot the latest of her husband's mistresses and left the body in his bed for him to find.

What perplex me are the dozen or so gaps in the album, spaces where photographs had once been displayed, but from which they have been removed. There are traces of gum and paper still visible where the photographs were wrenched out, and in several cases an inscription, viciously scored out. I can only guess that these are mementoes of some sort of scandal that happened in the late twenties or thirties. I'll mention it to my mother – there's a very slim chance that some of them have survived.

24

EDITED TRANSCRIPT OF TAPE-RECORDED NOTES
MADE BY MICHAEL FERARU (MIHAI VLĂHUŢA)

'Tape number two . . . er . . . twenty-seventh of November. More stuff for private consumption.

'Liliana's been a real help sorting through the photographs. Some of the inscriptions were in French, but most of them were in Romanian, and I wasn't always able to make sense of them. Her knowledge of immediate pre-Communist history's a little patchy – what she was taught in school wasn't exactly unbiased – but she makes up for that by her enthusiasm. Poking around in archives is getting to be a sort of passion with her, and she's done a terrific job so far of identifying various stuffed shirts in the Vlăhuţa rogues' gallery. Hey ho, we may have our own Vlad the Impaler, you never know my luck. I've handed her the bundle of letters mother sent, to see if there's anything interesting there.

'More to the point, she let me kiss her last night. It wasn't too serious, at least not on her part. We'd had a bit to drink, some God-awful local plonk, and we'd been horsing around a little, joking about my great-aunt Marthe, and the kiss . . . well, I don't know, I suppose it started as a sort of joke, but . . . the thing is, when I got a bit more interested, she just broke off and . . . For a couple of minutes, though, I don't think she was pretending, and as for me, I'm . . . well, I'm certain I'm in love with her, except, well . . . I just don't want to push her, and I don't want to take advantage of my position. For all I know, she may have someone else already . . . I'm seeing her tonight. If she's got a boyfriend, I'm sure she's bound to mention him then.'

25

Letter from Sophie Wandless to Michael Feraru (Mihai Vlăhuța) (received 28 November)

90 Mill Road
Cambridge

20 November

Dear Whatever-Your-Name-Is,

Michael, what's going on? You've hardly written in weeks, and you haven't actually replied to any of my letters. I know you're busy, and I know sorting things out in Bucharest can't be easy. But I am your girlfriend, and I think I deserve a little better than this. Or does absence make the heart grow less fond?

If you don't want me to come out at Christmas, just say so. I'd rather not spend the money and make such a long journey only to find at the end of it that you've gone off me or found someone else.

Your mother rang yesterday. I said I was planning to write, and she asked me to send you her love. She sounded a bit down. Said she hadn't been sleeping well. I think you'd better get a letter off to her as well while you're at it. Or perhaps you've found another mother as well as another woman.

I'm sorry, this must sound fairly petty. There you are, out in what I suppose we ought to call the Third World, working hard to open an orphanage, and here I am accusing you of infidelity and God knows what else. I should tear this letter up, but I suppose it won't do any harm if you can see just how badly all this is affecting me.

I spoke to Arthur Drewe about playing down the orphanage bit, and he said he'd do what he could. All the same, the project really does seem to mean a lot to him, and one of the senior boys – Jack Matthews – has made quite a personal thing of it. Drewe says it's too late to stop the boys travelling out there at Christmas. Apart from the personal disappointment, they've paid quite a hefty deposit on a minibus to carry out the various items they've succeeded in putting together. I'm sure it won't interfere too badly with what you're doing.

Old Drewe seemed a bit odd, mind you. Withdrawn, and not quite there. There were bags under his eyes – he looks as though he's been having a few sleepless nights as well.

Look, I'm sorry this hasn't been the cheeriest of letters. It's just that I miss you, and I do need some reassurance. I love you, for God's sake, and I wish I were with you right this moment. By the time I get to Bucharest, I think I'll either have burst with frustration or shrivelled up. I sincerely hope I'll find you in the same condition.

A whole aid-convoy-full of kisses,
Sophie

26

HEADMASTER'S ADDRESS TO THE MORNING ASSEMBLY, KING WILLIAM'S SCHOOL

28 November

It is my painful duty this morning to convey to all of you the sad news that one of our senior boys, Jack Matthews, was killed last night in a traffic accident while returning from a concert in the Arts Theatre. Two other boys, Alistair Bowen and Nigel Lamb, also members of the Upper Sixth, escaped with minor injuries and are due to leave hospital today.

In a moment, I shall ask you to bow your heads while we pray for Jack, his parents, and his younger brother Tom, who joined our first form only this term. But before that, it is only fitting that I should say a few words about Jack himself. He was, as most of you will be aware, an extremely popular boy, and I know he will be mourned by a large circle of friends. I shall remember him, not only as a keen rugby player, who brought honours to the first XV and to the school, but as a thoughtful boy who always had time to spare for others.

When I spoke this morning with Jack's House Master, Mr Spalding, there was one phrase he used several times: 'a good egg'. Now, I don't suppose many people use that expression nowadays, but the fact is, Jack Matthews was a very good egg. I don't want to give the wrong impression. Jack was not a goody-goody. Anything but. He was as lively a young man as I have met – and I've met more than my fair share – and as disrespectful of false authority the next man. He'd no time for cant or humbug, no room in his tragically short life for anything low or mean-spirited. And he was not the type to sit back and criticize what he couldn't put right himself.

Jack ran in marathons for a string of charities from Oxfam to the recent Rwanda Appeal: he was always ready to raise money for a good cause. His most recent project – a project he will not now see completed – was the King William's Romania Fund. Jack was the driving force behind the fundraising, and he was to have led the school expedition to Romania this coming vacation, carrying supplies to Mr Feraru's orphanage in Bucharest. Instead of spending Christmas with his family and friends, Jack was prepared to travel in the heart of winter to bring supplies to children in one of Europe's poorest countries. Now, tragically, he will not be going home for Christmas again.

I spoke early this morning with Mr Jay, the master who will be accompanying the expedition. He suggested two things, both of which I heartily endorse.

First, the trip to Romania will go ahead as planned, in Jack's honour. And, second, another fund, to be known as the Jack Matthews Memorial Fund, will be set up as a permanent focus for the collection of money for Romanian children.

And now, gentlemen, let us bow our heads, while the chaplain reads a short prayer for our departed friend Jack and all who loved him.

27

Notes from Liliana Popescu's 'Michael Feraru/Mihai Vlăhuţa' file
(Undated)

Since Casă Feraru incident, much disturbed. Nicu useless. Refuses to take any of it seriously. No one else to talk to, least of all Mihai. Need to find out more about Vlăhuţas.

Several days trawling through histories. Just finished Prodan's *Iobăgia în Transilvania în secolul al-XVII-lea*, both volumes. Good stuff on *boyar* history, but nothing startling. Ready to start work on his sixteenth-century volumes.

Discovered the *Bibliografia istorică a României* and Mircea's catalogue of manuscripts. Checking the national library for early material. Must read Cantemir's *Hronicul*. Got all I can from Prodan – seems to steer clear of the Vlăhuţas.

Only a couple of references in Cantemir, and nothing at all in Costin or Cantacuzino. I wonder is it worth it? I let Mihai kiss me last night. He wanted to go further, but I held back. Just. He's not as daft as I thought at first, and I do find him attractive. I said nothing about Nicu. Should I have?

Found a huge collection of papers on seventeenth-century *boyar* families, tucked away in the Biblioteca Centrala. Good index – already found half a dozen references to the Vlăhuţas.

Entire day spent reading material on Vlăhuţas. Extremely unsettling – no wonder chronicles say so little about them. Still can't see how it all ties in, though. Must read further.

What I found today – surely it can't be true? But if it is? I wonder if Mihai knows. Would his father have told him, or his grandfather? It turns my blood cold to think of it. Can anything be done to put an end to it all?

28

28 November

What a terrible day – the worst I can remember in such a long time.
Young Matthews's parents turned up just after lunch. I hadn't been
expecting them so soon, and it took me quite by surprise. They had
come to identify his body, of course, and take him back home for the
burial. Mrs Matthews was quite distraught. All they wanted was to
talk to me about their son – how he'd been getting on at school and
so on. I found it very difficult, though thankfully Jean was there to
help things along. She's a wonder with parents: knows how to put
them at their ease, even in a situation like that. I can't think how I'd
cope without her. We talked about the proposed Memorial Fund. That
seemed to help a lot, although I'm not really sure they were taking
much in.

It's time for bed, and I hope tomorrow will bring some good news.
The boys could do with some. The whole school has been thoroughly

subdued by Jack Matthews's death, and some of the senior boys are deeply upset. I don't think there'll be another Jack at the school for a long time.

I shall be alone tonight, for the first time in I cannot remember how many years. My wife has gone back to London with Mr and Mrs Matthews, in order to look after young Tom while they busy themselves with the funeral arrangements. Of course, we offered to keep the young lad at the school, but his parents seemed keen to have him with them, and I can't say I blame them. I shouldn't be surprised if they decide to withdraw him from school next term.

I'd give anything for Jean to be with me tonight. It's not just that I'm upset over the boy's death. If the chattering comes again, I hate to think there will be no one in this empty house with me.

4.20 a.m. Jabbering and talking all night. I have not slept a wink. The light has stayed on in the bedroom throughout, but it has made little difference. At about three o'clock, I fancied I could hear footsteps on the stairs. I sat in bed, rigid with fear and half mad with exhaustion, and in due course the sound receded. All the same, I do not think I am alone after all.

5.45 a.m. I must have fallen asleep about an hour ago. When I woke, something was in the room. I saw nothing, but I knew I was being watched. Watched and, in some sense, appraised. I thought I would go quite mad with the horror of it. The feeling lasted for perhaps five minutes, then I became aware that I was alone again. I must not sleep again at any cost.

6.30 a.m. It has spoken to me. I am writing this in the study, where I have been ever since the first visitation. My hand is shaking, and I can scarcely control the pen; but I need to set down my impressions now, for fear I do not have a chance later.

The dreadful thing, and what has upset me more than anything so far, is that it chose to speak to me in young Jack Matthews's voice, or, rather, in a simulacrum of it that was never quite accurate and that slipped at times into an ugly mumbling or an incoherent babble like the sounds I had heard previously on Bodley Stairs.

It has told me why it is here and what it wants from me. Dear God, what am I to do? It leaves me very little choice. But before I do anything else, I must write to Michael Feraru and warn him of the very great danger he is in. I must act now, before it returns.

29

Clipping from the *Cambridge Advertiser*, 30 November

DREWE, ARTHUR MERVIN, MA – 29 November, suddenly, at home. Late of King William's School. Greatly mourned by his wife Jean, his children Roger ('Little Man') and Denise, and grandchildren, Emma, Valerie, Terence, and Oliver, and by all members of staff and pupils of King William's, present and former. House private, family flowers only please. Funeral tomorrow, 1 December, from King William's School chapel (service, 2.00 p.m.), afterwards to City Cemetery, Newmarket Road for 3.30 p.m. God bless and keep him.

30

EDITED TRANSCRIPT OF TAPE-RECORDED NOTES
MADE BY MICHAEL FERARU (MIHAI VLĂHUȚA)

'It's November the twenty-seventh and I'm getting ready to go out. We're having a celebration, Liliana and I, that is. There's been really good news. My claim to Castel Vlaicu's been officially recognized, and I'm off there tomorrow for a first look round. The paperwork can wait till I get back. I don't want to lose the chance to get there because of bad weather.

'Liliana's agreed to come with me, though she's still behaving a bit oddly. She asked me yesterday if I had a birthmark near my right armpit. How on earth did she know? She seems worried about something. Perhaps our trip to the country will do her good. Not to mention myself.'

31

TELEGRAM FROM MRS ROSEMARY FERARU TO
MICHAEL FERARU (MIHAI VLĂHUŢA)

(Dated 29 November: marked 'recipient gone away')

RING IMMEDIATELY STOP BAD NEWS STOP
DISCOVERED LETTERS FROM FATHER STOP
YOU MUST NOT REPEAT MUST NOT GO TO
CASTEL VLAICU STOP WORRIED SICK STOP

Part II

---

castel vlaicu

1

Extract from the Journal of
Mihai Vlăhuţa

2 December

The cold never ends, never slackens, never gives the slightest respite. At times we are so cold, I think we will die from it. All day, we think only of how to keep warm, and in my dreams I fantasize, not about sex or food, but about hot sunshine and blazing fires. There have been moments in a sudden descent of icy rain when I have wished for death, seeing no other way out. The Carpathians are hell in reverse – ice for fire, sleet for coals, snow for flames.

2

Edited transcript of tape-recorded notes made by Mihai Vlăhuţa

'I've just been writing in my journal, . . . er . . . today, the second of December, but I've no real heart for it, not at the moment. I'll begin again later, I must be sure to set things down in writing. But this'll do for the moment.

'Our journey seems under some sort of curse already. Liliana and I left Bucharest four days ago. We got an *accelerat* train as far as Braşov, and then we changed to another one, headed for Miercurea-Ciuc, and after that, it . . . I don't know, it all sort of fell apart. There were some heavy snowfalls blocking the line after Sfîntu Gheorghe, and we all had to get out. The station-master suggested we take a branch line train as far as . . . what's the bloody place called? Hang on . . .

[PAUSE.]

'Right, a place called Tîrgu Secuiesc. The idea was to take a bus from there to Oneşti, then a train west to our original destination. It seemed a bloody long way round.

'Anyway, one hour later, and there we were on board a wretched little *cursă*, huffing and puffing its way out of Sfîntu Gheorghe as though it meant business; but we'd scarcely gone a few miles to Brateş when it became obvious we just weren't going to make it. There was more snow ahead, and talk of a rockfall past Covasna. Every time we looked out of the window, the air seemed to be thick with snow. I could scarcely believe it when I saw these frigging icicles hanging from the carriage roof. We could see others on the branches of the trees, ten or twenty feet long some of them.

'To tell the truth, I almost thought of turning back and getting the next train to Bucharest, but that would have meant giving up all hope of getting to Castel Vlaicu till spring, and I'm afraid I just wasn't prepared to risk that. I made up my mind that I'd find a way through if I could, and Liliana agreed. I think she regrets it now, though. In fact, I think she's afraid we're going to die out here in the mountains. But there's no going back. Not now. We've committed ourselves. We must find Castel Vlaicu or perish.'

3

Extract from the Journal of Mihai Vlăhuţa

2 December

We spent the first night in Brateş, in a farmer's house. It was my first experience of the Romanian countryside. I'd heard and read of the warmth and hospitality of ordinary Romanians in the villages, how they welcomed foreigners with open arms, how they had somehow managed to escape the worst effects of those long years of Communist rule. But, to be frank, I did not find them so. They received us grudgingly, and demanded payment for our food and board. Perhaps it was Liliana's presence. Perhaps it was because I was introduced as Mihai. Perhaps the endemic corruption of the new regime has achieved what years under Ceauşescu could not.

It was bitterly cold, and Liliana and I were unceremoniously bundled into the hayloft for the night. The rest of the family – the skinny farmer, his dumpy wife, their four sons and three daughters – occupied the other rooms. I envied the boys their huge four-poster bed in one corner of the kitchen, the warmest place in the house. Liliana and I were treated as man and wife, and we thought it best not to draw attention to our true status. We slept next to one another, but remained fully clothed.

I have never spent a more uncomfortable night. The hay – which had its share of inhabitants – prickled my skin even through the blankets, and the cold was terrible. The one bright spot came when, through the darkness, Liliana reached out her hand for mine and held it tightly until the cold forced us both to let go and bring our freezing fingers back beneath the thin covers. I woke after dreams of ice and snow; but buried at the heart of them lay an imprecise, ill-formulated image of Liliana's face.

I noticed last night that she has brought the doll with her, the one I found in Casă Feraru.

Yesterday, having woken and breakfasted early, we paid our surly hosts and set off to find the one garage Brateş had to offer. It was a rundown affair with a single pump and a low-roofed workshop from which the sound of banging and scraping emerged from time to time. No one came at first, in spite of our calls, and we were forced to push our way into the workshop. We found the owner there, a short, bad-tempered Székely called Laszlo. He did nothing to improve our opinion of the local population.

At first, Laszlo denied outright that he had any vehicles for sale or hire, but Liliana nagged him until he owned up to keeping an old Dacia in the back. The car – a 1400 cc Romanian version of a Renault 12 – was in a rotten state of repair, he protested, not worth the trouble of putting on the road, a potential hazard to man or beast. And I have to confess that, when we first clapped eyes on it, we were inclined to concur. On closer examination, however, it showed signs of having been left in that condition quite deliberately, probably to avoid some obscure tax or requisition by the state. We made him get it out and start it up, and once it got going the engine sounded quite healthy – for a Dacia.

In the end, Laszlo agreed to hire the car out for what seemed an absurdly high price. But I was desperate by then and agreed to pay what he asked, as much to get away from the man as anything. He had a permanent scowl that seemed to have been moulded onto his face at birth, his voice whined like his car, and his manner left me in no doubt as to his opinion of me.

I could not get to the bottom of his reluctance to hire the car out, though, considering how much he made from the transaction in the end. Perhaps he just wasn't interested in money. But Liliana thinks that, in common with many villagers, he's unwilling to accept that much, if anything, has changed since the revolution, and that entrusting his property to a couple of strangers was tantamount to giving it away.

We arranged by telephone for someone to drive the car back from Baraolt, which was about as far as we could get into the mountains by car, and by late morning we set off in a cloud of exhaust fumes and grating gears.

4

EDITED TRANSCRIPT OF TAPE-RECORDED NOTES
MADE BY MIHAI VLĂHUȚA

'It's still the second of December and I'm bloody worried, to be honest. Look, I . . . The thing is . . . Damn . . .

[PAUSE.]

'Look, I don't see us coming out of this alive, and . . . the fact is, I can't write about it, it's not even . . .

'The funny thing is, I'm not frightened, at least not . . . frightened of dying out here. I can't explain, it's . . . I am feeling guilty about Liliana, though, dropping her into this and everything. And, oh, I don't know, I feel bad about Sophie actually, and the fact she doesn't know what's going on, and when she . . . Oh, shit, well, when she finds out . . .

'Of course, she may just think I've disappeared, which could be worse, really. And then there's my mother. I do feel rotten about her, especially after what happened to father. But . . . well, as I said, I don't feel the least bit frightened. In a way, I almost feel I'm being looked after, or that I will be. As if . . . oh, God, I don't know . . . as if I'm important for some reason. Does that make any sense? Hang on, Liliana's coming back in . . .'

5

Extract from the Journal of Mihai Vlăhuţa

3 December

The journey went well enough at first. I was entranced by the road, tree-bordered and virtually traffic free. It seemed to be leading us deeper and deeper into a world that has all but vanished everywhere else. The only other vehicles we passed were horse-drawn carts of one sort or another. Once, at a crossroads, we saw a shepherd in a fleece cloak that fell to his ankles, wearing a tall black hat, and looking for all the world as though he had just stepped out of a picture-book from 1920 or earlier. He watched us pass with what seemed a look of bewilderment, as though he had never seen a motorcar before. Perhaps he had not.

We passed through quiet villages with houses strung out along long streets, very different to the Saxon hamlets we had seen from the train after Braşov. The houses sat end on to the road, and behind them stood huge barns as high as three-storey houses at home. Almost every house had its own gateposts, elaborately carved and painted.

At one place we halted for a late lunch, a simple meal of coarse bread and *slănină,* washed down with cups of sweet tea, for, in spite of its name, the *cofetăria* sold no coffee.

Once, as we ate, I noticed an old woman staring at me as though she recognized me, or had seen a ghost. She was a wizened old creature, dressed in old-fashioned clothes, her limbs knotted and bent with age and arthritis, her skin mottled with dark liver spots.

I was reminded of something my mother had often told me, that I bore a close resemblance to my father when he was young. I wondered if, by some curious chance, the crone had seen or even known him at that age. We were not yet in Vlăhuţa country, but I knew that my father and other members of my family had travelled widely through the countryside. In the end, the old woman's stare made me so uneasy I turned my back as well as I could and continued with my meal.

As we were leaving, we had to pass her table. I went ahead to pay, and, as Liliana passed, the old woman beckoned to her. I saw them as I stood waiting by the door, Liliana with her head bent down to catch what the bent little creature was saying. They remained thus for a minute or so, then I saw Liliana pull away as though shocked or hurt, and come towards me quickly.

As we stepped outside, I turned to her.

'What was all that about?' I asked.

'Nothing,' she answered, 'nothing. Just superstitious talk. Old women in these villages have nothing better to do.'

However much I pressed her, she would not tell me what the old woman had said, though I could see it had troubled her. She still refuses to tell me, and I have stopped asking. Did the old woman ask my name? Or tell Liliana that a ghost was walking through that cold, wood-panelled room?

* * *

The chief drawback to our car was its lack of a heater. Or, to be more precise, the absence of a heater that worked. Fiddle as we might with the knobs, the little *calorifer* stubbornly resisted all efforts to extract even a trickle of warmth. We kept our thick winter coats on, and got out every so often to reinvigorate our circulation. The temperature was low, and it dropped yet further as we moved higher into the mountains.

We began to realize how poorly equipped we had come for our journey. The Harghita Mountains are cold and empty and unforgiving, and we had entered them as though going on a picnic. We had our coats and our cases, and that was all. After Brăduţ there were no more villages, and the road became a track. By late afternoon, it had grown dark, and heavy snow had started to fall, obliterating the track and slowing us to a crawl. The Dacia was not built for such conditions. With every bend, the track became steeper, and I knew it would not be much longer before the little engine gave out.

'I think we should turn back,' said Liliana once, but I knew it was already too late for that. I simply could not risk the descent in the darkness, knowing that a skid could take us out of control and over the edge. I pushed the car on, hoping the path would flatten out, but it did not.

We got another mile or so before the engine finally wheezed to a halt. The silence that followed in its wake was so dense I thought I could hear the snow land on the roof and windscreen. We sat without speaking for a very long time, knowing we might be mere hours from certain death.

I touched her then, deliberately, my hand grazing her cheek, then stroking it, and she said nothing all the time, but looked me full in the face, in the eyes, as though locking me there with her gaze. In the end, I put my hand behind her head and drew her face to mine and

106

kissed her, and this time she did not resist. We kissed for a long time, and she did not break away, and my tongue entered her mouth, and at last her tongue entered mine. When we stopped at last, far short of what we wanted, it was still dark outside, and the cold was like knives. All sounds had halted, smothered in snow. Such silence, such cold, such longing.

'We have to get out of here,' I said finally. 'If we stay in the car, we'll die.'

'We could sleep in the back. We have clothes in our cases.'

I shook my head.

'People die in cars. By morning we may be snowed in. We have to go.'

'Go where?'

I hesitated. Where indeed?

'This track has to lead somewhere. A farm, a shepherd's hut – we have to try.'

'We could go back.'

I shook my head.

'We'd never make it. There were dips at the foot of the track, they'll be full of snow by now. We have to go on.'

She had grown up in milder countryside than this. The darkness and the driving snow frightened her, those and the unforgiving reputation of the Harghita range. The car seemed safe for the moment, but I knew it was a death trap. It took me a while, but I persuaded her in the end.

We left most of our belongings behind in the cases, wearing only what we could actually put on without unduly hampering our movements. Liliana brought the doll: she said she could not bear to part with it. Our one stroke of luck was that we had brought two torches and batteries. I had Liliana to thank for them: she had explained that no Romanian train has lights in the carriages, and in winter a long journey can be unbearably tedious without a torch to read by. I slipped the batteries into my coat pocket and gripped my torch as though it was the only remaining link between us and the world of light.

The moment we stepped outside, we were enveloped in snow. It was no longer drifting down, but rushing at us, driven by high winds that blew uninterrupted through an unseen pass ahead. Our feet sank eighteen inches or more into deep snow, making forward progress difficult and tiring. We started to trudge forward, keeping to the path by guesswork more than anything. The beam of the torch bounced back off the curtain of snowflakes in front, making it impossible to see anything but a swirling mass of white. It was almost as though the light had attracted a swarm of ice-cold moths, and I put my arm up in front of my face to ward them off, as if I feared they would devour me.

We lost track of time and distance alike, trudging ahead, bent over, our bodies numb with cold and limp with exhaustion. It may have been half an hour, it may have been hours, I really cannot say. All I know is that we went on walking through the snow like two injured animals going to slaughter. I think we would have died if we'd carried on like that very much longer. We were very near our limits.

The path suddenly levelled out, and I knew we had come to the top of a path or ridge. Casting about desperately for some sort of shelter, we stumbled across what I had prayed against all odds to find – a hunter's *cabana*, set just off the track, at the edge of deep forest.

We forced the weakly padlocked door and staggered inside. The sound of the door slamming behind us, shutting out the worst of the wind, is the most beautiful thing I have ever heard.

We spent a long time just sitting, shivering, catching our breath, and coming back to our senses. We were still in danger, for the temperature inside the *cabana* was only marginally above that outside, and it was still cold enough to kill us. All the same, it was tempting to stay sitting there until sleep overpowered me. Had I done so, I would not have wakened again.

When I finally had the strength to move about again, my first concern was to find a lamp. In the end, I discovered an old kerosene light. Liliana extricated a matchbox from beneath her several layers of outer clothing, and I watched her put a flame to the wick with a trembling hand. It was the most wonderful thing in the world to see the light hold and rise, and to watch a soft glow spread out through the little hut as I replaced the glass lampshade over the flame. Liliana smiled nervously at me, and I smiled back. It was as though we had both come back from the dead.

With the lamp lit, I could explore the little cabin at leisure. I looked for food, but although I found a can opener, there were no cans, not a morsel of any description. My next concern was firewood, and to my delight I found a stack of it next to the old cast-iron stove that took up the centre of the room. I cleared the grate, filled the cavity with little sticks and larger logs, then got the thing going with the aid of a rag soaked in kerosene. Within minutes, there was a roaring fire, and warmth, and a feeling of inexpressible peace and contentment.

It was then that I kissed Liliana again, and this time, when she responded, we had no cause to hold back. All the fears and uncertainties of the past few hours went into our lovemaking, and when we slept at last, we were like children coming out of the dark to a new and unsuspected light.

I woke once, my body close to Liliana's, my head throbbing in the stuffy heat that filled the *cabana*. Something had woken me. I listened carefully, hearing nothing at first but the whine of the wind outside. My stomach was empty, and I thought perhaps hunger had broken my sleep. Then I heard a sound that, for all its banality, sent shivers racing across the surface of my naked skin. Somewhere, a wolf was howling in the darkness, and its voice was the loneliest thing I had ever heard, a forlorn cry launched into that white, unpeopled emptiness outside.

Liliana had spoken to me a couple of times about wolves. For some reason, Romanians, even today, have an unreasoning horror of them and bears. Certainly, their forests are among the last to be inhabited by these creatures, and their fear has much to do with the havoc the wolves wreak on sheep and other livestock. During our drive, I had noticed several bark-bound fences, eight-foot high or more, that were, Liliana told me, built for no other purpose than to keep wolves at bay. And the shepherd I had seen at the crossroads had been accompanied by a large dog, its thick spiked collar designed as a protection against the same threat.

Liliana had tried to reassure me, saying few humans were ever attacked. Rationally, I knew she was right, and even in that exposed cabin in the mountains I was certain we would come to no physical harm from the wolves outside. But as I listened to the creature howling, its voice rising and falling through the emptiness of snow and ice, I understood something that had seemed meaningless in the city: that my people did not fear the wolf because it might tear out their throats, but because it wandered wild out here in places almost beyond the reach of death itself.

Liliana sensed my restlessness and woke as well, clinging to me for extra warmth. I half expected her to make a joke about the wolf, as she had done back in Bucharest, to say something about 'the children of the night'. But she just lay there still, without speaking, as though waiting for dawn to come. It was a long time coming, but I do not think either of us slept again.

* * *

We got up soon after first light and got the fire blazing properly again. Our friendly wolf had deserted us by then, but the sound of wind had not diminished.

The euphoria we had felt on first finding the *cabana* evaporated quickly once we took full stock of our situation. Without food, we could not stay where we were. The *cabana* was clearly not used at this time of year, and there was absolutely no point in hanging on just in case a hunter happened to drop by. How far we could get before succumbing to the cold or exhaustion exacerbated by hunger was anyone's guess, but it wasn't likely to be more than a few miles.

One thing that did raise our spirits was finding a couple of pairs of snow shoes on a shelf. With them, Liliana explained, we could make much faster progress and even cross tracts of deep snow. We found a sack, and into it we piled various bits and pieces that we thought might come in handy: as many logs as we could carry, some kerosene, a pot in which to melt snow for drinking water, a rusty knife, a length of rope, the spare torch and batteries, and the can opener, just in case. The doll went in as well: it had become a sort of mascot, and Liliana refused to leave it. I have grown to dislike it. There's something sinister about it, something uncanny. I wish I had not given it to her.

6

EDITED TRANSCRIPT OF TAPE-RECORDED NOTES
MADE BY MIHAI VLĂHUŢA

'It's time to leave, though we're both reluctant to give up our warm haven. It's still the third of December. I've just finished writing up my journal in a sort of . . . well, I don't know, a mood of defiance. I don't imagine I'll live to re-read it, let alone use it for the book I was going to write. I've never felt so wretched. All that stuff about being looked after! What a load of crap. You wake up next morning, and there you are – "same as it ever was", as David Byrne puts it.

'A bath and a shave and a good meal wouldn't go amiss, but I've as much chance of those as I have of meeting David Byrne. I'm still feeling guilty about Sophie. She needn't ever know about last night, of course. What's it matter anyway? Eh? I'll be dead if she does ever find out. But I do know now I'm really in love with Liliana, and if we do come out of this alive, I'll have to tell Sophie. Assuming Liliana still wants me, of course – last night wasn't exactly ordinary.

'I've been having a look through the windows. The wind's dropped a bit, but there's a lot of snow out there, and it's still coming down steadily. We're surrounded by dark spruce forests. Just look at them. You could get lost in there and never see daylight again. The track from the cabin seems to go down through a steep gorge to the next valley. The entire region looks as if it's empty of people. I haven't even heard an aeroplane going over. There's something unnerving about the thought that we may die in perfect silence.'

7

Extract from the Journal of
Mihai Vlăhuţa

3 December, late evening

We are alive, though only just. All around us, the silence continues to grow, but there are voices too. Liliana and I are not alone.

We seemed to have left the real world and entered a realm which had no reality, a realm in which we appeared to be the only living things. Soon after leaving the cabin, I saw a waterfall hanging across a gorge that seemed to have no bottom. It was frozen, every last droplet of water in it held fast as though sheathed in glass, shimmering for hundreds of feet until it was at last lost from sight. A little further, we passed a mountain stream that had been turned to ice. The forest stood on every side, dark and impenetrable, a place of shadows and watching eyes.

Without the snow shoes, we would certainly have died. From time to time, one of us would look up and see a mass of compacted snow hanging from the rocks above, as though about to tip and fall. A loud noise, perhaps the mere snapping of a twig would have brought it crashing down, white and formless, to bury us until spring. Or perhaps spring never comes to those high places of snow and ice.

After a while, the path was not hard to trace. We were hemmed in on both sides by high stone walls pillared with icicles. The snow was falling vertically now, making visibility difficult, but we were grateful not to have the wind to chill us even further.

We reached the bottom at last, and ahead of us we could see a valley widening out. Our strength was already sapped, and Liliana said she could walk no further. I knew it was dangerous to stop, but I was in as bad a state as she was. We stopped and lit a small fire. I used the knife to cut some twigs from a tree, but they were too green to burn, and threatened to put out what fire we had.

We continued to walk in short stages, but we were growing seriously hungry now, and weak. Sometime after noon, it stopped snowing, but the sky above remained leaden and threatening. It was warmer here than on the pass, but we both knew that if we did not find food and shelter soon, we would have to accept the inevitable.

We had completely lost our bearings by then. The little map I had brought from Bucharest was wholly useless. None of the villages we had gone through after Brateş was shown on it, and the road we had followed had been so twisting it was impossible to say exactly where we had ended up. With the sun permanently shrouded in thick cloud, there wasn't even an approximate means of determining which way was east or which west. Any markers there might have been to point out trails to foresters or hikers would have been obliterated beneath the snow.

Liliana saw the first wolf about an hour after we had started walking along the valley floor. There was a frozen stream on our right and dense forest to our left, made up of sycamore, birch, beech, and yet more spruce. Liliana saw a flicker of something moving between the

115

trees, and told me to look. I saw nothing at first, then half a mile later, there it was, a flash of grey, moving like a whisper among the snow-bound trunks. A second followed it, then a third. They were pacing us, waiting for us to stumble or rest. Once, glancing round, I saw cold bright eyes watching us from the shadows. When I shook my hand, they flickered and were gone.

'They're frightened of us,' I said. 'For all they know, we're hunters. We could have guns.'

Liliana said nothing, but I could see that my reassurances carried little weight with her. Her fear went deeper than the physical. More than guns would have been needed to chase away her demons, but all we had for weapons were a rusty knife and a half-empty bottle of kerosene.

The wolves posed a serious threat. I had been holding in reserve the possibility of taking refuge in the forest if all else failed. It would be relatively sheltered in there, and we might be able to find enough dead wood with which to build a fire that would see us through to morning. There would have been little point in entering the forest before nightfall, however – as long as it continued light, we had to make what progress we could in the slim hope of finding some sort of habitation.

But my chief reason for not seeking shelter among the trees had been a fear that, once inside, we might never find our way out again. Now, the risk of being stalked by wolves made the forest less attractive.

We went on for another hour or more, taking only the briefest of halts, never long enough to make the wolves think we were starting to tire. But all the time we knew our strength was ebbing. I knew we would have to reach a decision soon. Once it was dark, it would be too late to risk the trees. We would have to go in there while there was still enough light to collect wood by. Our torches would not be sufficient on their own to frighten off the wolves, and it would have been foolish to waste the batteries.

That was when we heard a sound in the distance, a shuddering, echoing sound that seemed to come from all directions at once. We halted, holding our breaths, straining to make it out.

'Someone's chopping down a tree,' exclaimed Lilian, unable to keep the excitement out of her voice.

'Are you sure?'

'Yes, yes – quite sure. Listen.'

The sound came again, steady now, with a ring to it that spoke of steel biting into wood. Moments later, the chopping gave way to cracking, then the tearing and flapping of a tree as it crashed through the branches of its neighbours. A last crash shivered the forest as it struck the ground.

Silence rushed back in as if to repair the wound left by the crash; it seemed no longer threatening, but filled with the promise of rescue and safety. Liliana called aloud, and a moment later I joined her, both of us shouting and yelling as though we had suddenly gone quite mad. A minute or two later, a man shuffled out of the forest ahead of us, stumbling on to the path and looking round wildly to see who was responsible for the uproar.

We hurried towards him as best we could, sending up little flurries of snow in our haste. I tripped and fell once, winding myself and bruising my knees. The man made no movement in our direction. As we approached him, we expected some sort of greeting, some indication that he was aware of our presence, but he stared expressionlessly at us until we were right beside him. Liliana spoke first, stretching out her hand as she did so, but without awakening an answering gesture on the man's part.

He was a stockily built man of late middle age, dressed in traditional peasant clothes, with a black sheepskin hat and a long moustache that had started to turn grey. In his right hand, he held a broad-bladed axe, and in his belt sat a long-handled knife. The frozen skirts of his long coat grazed the surface of the snow. He listened without response as Liliana continued to explain our predicament. I thought he might be Hungarian, that it was useless speaking Romanian to him. But when Liliana came to a halt, he answered her in her own language, spoken in a thick Transylvanian accent.

'I am here to cut wood,' he said. If I do not bring wood back to the village, my wife and children will freeze.'

'What village?' Liliana asked. 'Is it far?'

He shook his head.

'When I have finished, I will take you there. Wait for me here.'

A moment later, he had returned to the forest. Soon, we heard the sound of further chopping as he started on the task of cutting his tree into manageable segments. We waited, growing colder all the time, but reluctant to risk losing our one chance of safety in a hunt for the village. It started to snow again, and we stepped into shelter beneath the nearest trees. A few small flakes threaded their way down through the branches. We would watch them flutter and touch the ground and vanish. The trees were rimed with thick white frost, as though eternally frozen. Not many steps further on, the darkness began, as though it would go on for ever. Several times I saw eyes looking out at us, and once a grey shape flitted past and was lost again.

Our man returned at last, dragging behind him a low sledge loaded with freshly cut logs. He pulled it with the help of a sort of leather harness. Seeing us still waiting, he beckoned, then set off along the path. We hurried to catch up with him.

'I won't wait for you,' he said. 'I must get back before dark.'

I looked up and saw that the afternoon had worn on and that sunset was not far off. At least this must mean that the village was near at hand. We made an effort to keep up with our guide, and from time to time one or the other of us would endeavour to engage him in conversation, with little success.

Sometimes, he would pause and glance behind him, as though afraid he was being followed. I watched him do this several times, and in the end I could not restrain my curiosity any longer.

'Why do you keep looking round?' I asked. 'Are you expecting someone?'

He did not answer. We went on walking, and above us the sky was growing darker by the minute. Our guide quickened his pace, and we were starting to find it hard to keep up with him.

'We have torches,' I said. 'If it gets dark we can use them.'

He said nothing, but continued to push ahead. The only sounds were the crunching noise of our snow shoes and the hissing of the little sledge. Liliana stumbled, and I called out to the woodsman to halt while I helped her to her feet, but he did not falter in his step. Above the trees, the sunlight was leaching from the clouds.

Suddenly, I saw a light ahead, then another. We must have reached the village. Minutes later, we could make out the first building, a low barn set in the heart of a wide clearing, where the forest seemed to have been cut back on all sides. A dog came running out to greet our strange friend, and he stopped to pat it and hold it back from attacking us.

The sight of home seemed to have mellowed and calmed him.

'I'm sorry,' he said, 'to have made you walk so fast. It does not do to be outside after dark.'

'I'm surprised you go out alone even during the day, especially into the forest. Aren't you afraid the wolves may attack you?'

He stared at me as though I had said something unutterably stupid.

119

'Wolves?' he asked. 'What wolves?'

'We saw dozens of them in the forest,' I said. 'Slinking past, watching us, waiting for us to collapse.'

His face, which had relaxed a little, now tensed again. He turned and started to drag the sledge again, then paused and looked directly at me.

'You must have been mistaken,' he said. 'There are no wolves in this stretch of the mountains. There never have been.'

We have been in Silistraru several hours now. In the short time between our arrival and the onset of darkness, I managed to see a little of the place. The village is small, just a circle of one-storey houses in a side-valley, with a tiny wooden church in the centre that seems to date from the fourteenth century. I mean to pay it a visit tomorrow, before we leave.

Though reserved, the villagers are hospitable enough. Cut off here in their little valley, they probably see few outsiders from one year's end to the next. There are few signs that anything much has changed here in centuries. Our story about the car produced puzzled looks from more than one of our listeners. The people dress and act as though the twentieth century had passed them by completely. Our torches created a terrific sensation. There is no electricity here, no telephone, no television, no radio. The most modern things I have seen are some photographs on the wall of our host's home – and they seem about a hundred years old.

We have been taken in for the night by our woodsman, who turns out to be called Tamas, and his wife, a pleasant woman by the name of Ana. Once he settled in at home, Tamas relaxed considerably. He will never qualify for the title of 'the world's most talkative man', but he has done his best to put us at our ease. Caught totally unawares by our arrival, Ana rustled up a very palatable meal for us – triple helpings of a thick *ciorbă de perişoare*, followed by a large plate of hot *gogoaşî*, the delicious doughnuts my father used to insist my mother make for him. The yeast came from one neighbour, the sugar from another, so I know we were being specially favoured. We finished them to the last crumb.

Afterwards we drank cherry *ţuica* and talked. From time to time, a neighbour would call to get a good look at us and ask a few questions about the world outside. They seemed famished for news. Tamas had heard of England, but his general concept of geography was eccentric, to say the least, and I had the impression he thought I came from somewhere in Russia.

Though Liliana and I were both weary and in desperate need of sleep, our presence was too great a novelty to pass by without at least a peek. People came in dribs and drabs all evening, and I began to think we would never get to bed. There seemed to be a sort of pecking order, with the village elders calling first, and later the youngsters, none of whom seemed to be under twenty. These latter, men and women both, were inevitably the keenest to know about goings-on in the world outside. There were no children, or at least none were brought to see us.

By about ten o'clock, my head was spinning from the combined effects of tiredness, conversing for hours in Romanian, and the powerful local spirit. Tamas would never take 'no' for an answer, and as often as I emptied my little glass, he would refill it with a grin. I learned to sip more slowly, but my attempts to push the glass away were met with a frown and renewed efforts to get me drunk.

Our last visitor, in reverse order to established precedent, was the most important – the village priest, Father Gherasim. He is an ascetic-looking man of forty or so, with a long grey-flecked beard and the most piercing blue eyes I have ever seen.

He has been in Silistraru fifteen years now: he was sent there originally by the Metropolitan Bishopric in Cluj-Napoca when his predecessor, Father Mircea, died. Mircea, a villlage *popa* of the old school, uneducated and worldly, had served his tiny parish for fifty years or more. Gherasim, a young man with ambition at the time of his appointment, went to Silistraru with the intention of making one or two reputation-enhancing changes before moving on to somewhere less remote.

In time, however, the Bishopric forgot about him, and he adapted to the pattern of life in the village. He soon gave up his schemes for this or that innovation, and was in the end content to go on sleeping out his life in peace and quiet with the rest of his flock.

Father Gherasim had, I sensed, become a meditative man, more monk than priest, given to introspection and long, silent vigils. He was uninterested in news of events in the world outside. Recent happenings in Bucharest or London were of no concern to him. He affected not to have heard of the revolution, and merely nodded politely when Liliana told him of it. I couldn't work out if he was telling the truth or not.

He was more interested in us and what had brought us to the Harghita Mountains.

'What is your final destination?' he asked.

'We're looking for a place called Castel Vlaicu,' I said. 'Have you heard of it?'

Gherasim's expression did not change, nor did his eyes leave mine; but I saw something flicker in them, deep down, almost out of sight. Long moments passed before he answered.

'Yes,' he said. 'I have heard of it. Why do you wish to go there?'

I glanced round. The room was very quiet. I saw Tamas and Ana looking at me with an expression of what seemed very like alarm.

'To reclaim it as mine,' I said. 'I am Count Mihai Vlăhuţa. Castel Vlaicu is my home.'

I said the words almost in mockery of myself. Certainly, I had never felt less like a count, less ready to come into an inheritance. I thought Gherasim would dismiss me as a half-mad waif dragged out of the snow, laying claim to a castle he had never even set eyes on. He did not smile or laugh, however, but just went on looking at me with the same gravity as before.

'How will you get there?' he asked.

'I don't know. There doesn't seem to be much point in trying to get back to our car. We don't even know how far the castle is, or in which direction.'

'It's not far,' Gherasim said. 'A day's journey at most. But you will need a guide: you will never make it alone.'

'I'd be willing to pay if you know someone willing to help,' I said. It was hard to believe my luck, that I had come so close to my destination in spite of my misfortunes. But I was puzzled. For all his apparent helpfulness, the priest's tone was stern, almost disapproving. I wondered what I had said to offend him. Was it the mere fact that I was a count? If Castel Vlaicu was that close to Silistraru, perhaps the people here had memories of my family, bad memories from the days before reform.

He shook his head briefly.

'Tamas will take you. There will be no need for money. You should both be ready to leave first thing in the morning.'

He stood abruptly and bowed slightly, first to me, then to Liliana. There seemed to be no trace of irony in the gesture. His beard and long black robes bestowed on him a dignity and seriousness that raised him above such petty actions. As he turned to leave, he hesitated. His expression made me very uneasy.

'Tell me,' he said, 'what do you expect to find at Castel Vlaicu?'

'I've no idea,' I replied. 'My father and grandfather never talked about it. I imagine it's badly ruined. I'm not even sure if anyone's living there now.'

He looked at me oddly, and I saw that flicker in his eyes again.

'No, the castle is not entirely ruined. Some people still live there. Some of them may have known your grandfather.'

'Is anything wrong?' I asked, for I sensed there was something unspoken, a warning or a threat, something Father Gherasim wanted to say but would not or could not.

'You are a Vlăhuţa,' he said. 'You should know that better than I.'

'I don't understand.' I looked at Liliana, thinking that she, perhaps, might grasp whatever hidden meanings were intended; but she just looked dumbly at me and said nothing. She too, I sensed, knew something I did not.

'When you get to Castel Vlaicu you will understand,' said the priest, and with that he turned and left, shutting the door of the cottage hard.

All Tamas's eager hospitality seemed to have evaporated. Screwing the cap down on the *ţuica* bottle, he made his apologies and said we would have to get to bed straight away, since we were to be up and off soon after first light. I did not argue. Sleep was already washing over me, and it was all I could do to stay awake another moment.

Liliana and I have just been shown to a small side room, where Ana has prepared warm bedding. She seems ill at ease with me now, very different to the convivial woman who served dinner. I am writing my journal before I doze off, in order to be certain I have set down everything as it happened, but my eyes are shutting. Beside me, Liliana has already fallen into a deep sleep.

8

EDITED TRANSCRIPT OF TAPE-RECORDED NOTES MADE BY MIHAI VLĂHUŢA

'I woke about fifteen minutes ago, still in Tamas's house. It was just after midnight . . . still dark. Cold too . . . really cold . . . Liliana was still asleep. I was groggy . . . almost went straight back to sleep . . . only . . . I was sure . . . I thought I could hear something outside.

'I pulled the shutter aside and looked out. It had stopped snowing, and there was a large moon over the mountains. It was shining brightly down on the village square. I was . . . I don't know exactly . . . it was strange. Some of the villagers were walking towards the church . . . one, two at a time. I could just make out voices raised in a sort of chant. It reminded me of the Orthodox prayers I used to listen to when I was a child, when my grandparents took me to church. A midnight Mass? But what was it in aid of?

'I kept on watching as they slipped inside the building. I think most of the village was in there. I could see lights flickering through the windows, but that's all. I was really tempted to sneak outside: I wanted to see if I could snatch a glimpse of the proceedings, but . . . I don't know, something told me the villagers mightn't take too well to an outsider being there.

'I decided to go back to bed, it was so bloody cold I couldn't stand it any longer. And then . . . I heard another sound, just over the drone of the prayers: a wolf's howl. It sounded really sad and lonely, just drifting down to the village from somewhere out there in the forest. A couple of latecomers paused on their way to the church and looked round. So I knew they could hear it too, it wasn't my imagination. And then the howling died down, and they hurried into the church. I've heard nothing since.'

9

Extract from the Journal of Mihai Vlăhuţa

4 December

A strange thing happened this morning. Ana woke us shortly after dawn. It was still terribly cold, and, although a fire burned in the hearth, the cottage was not much warmer at that time than the outside. Our hosts seemed morose, and their red-rimmed eyes showed that they too had had little sleep during the night. I thought it prudent not to ask about the midnight Mass I had observed.

Tamas was in an outhouse, getting things ready for our journey. In the kitchen, Ana had prepared a breakfast of bread and herbal tea. While she and Liliana talked, I excused myself and went outside. The snow was still holding off, but a stiff breeze came down the valley, freezing everything in its path. In the sky, a few pale stars struggled against the onset of day; the moon had vanished altogether.

I wandered across the square to the little church, with its single tower and sloping, shingled roof. Churches have always been an interest of mine, but I've had little opportunity to visit any since arriving in Romania. This was a brief opportunity to see inside a village church that had every appearance of being among the oldest in the country.

I headed for the low door in the west wall, but as I approached, it opened, almost as though it had been operated by sensors. Father Gherasim appeared in the opening. He was tall and thin-faced and grim this morning, with long lines deeply etched in his forehead and cheeks. His eyes seemed sleepy, as though he had been up all night in prayer.

I greeted him and said I had come to pay a visit to his church before leaving. He shook his head and stepped outside, shutting the door behind him.

'I'm sorry,' he said, 'but I can't let you inside. It is not permitted.'

'Not permitted? I don't understand. Not permitted by whom?'

'By me. Please, it will soon be time for you to go.'

Ordinarily, I think I would have objected, but something in the priest's manner made me pause. It would do me no good to get into an argument with a man who had effective power of life and death while I was here.

I said nothing further, and turned to go. As I stepped away, however, Father Gherasim called my name.

'Mihai.'

I turned back to him. He was holding something out to me on the palm of his hand.

'This is for you,' he said. 'I want you to take it with you. It is very valuable. Please take great care of it.'

I stepped up to him and looked at the object in his outstretched hand. It was a small icon, encrusted with gold and silver, and obviously extremely old.

'I can't take this,' I said. It was a most beautiful object, depicting the Virgin in the classic pose of Hodigitria or Guide, with the Christ Child seated on her left arm, while she pointed to him with her right. I guessed that it had originally come from Russia.

'It will guarantee you a safe journey,' said Gherasim. 'And after that . . .' His voice faltered. 'Please take it,' he said.

There was such intensity of persuasion in his voice that, in spite of my reluctance, I stretched out my hand and lifted the icon. It felt strangely heavy. He handed me a leather pouch on a cord and instructed me to place the icon inside and to wear it on my neck, inside my clothes. I did as he said. The icon is there now, as I sit writing.

I thanked him awkwardly. He shook my hand and went back inside the church. I caught only a glimpse of the interior as he entered, a muted flashing of gold in shadow. Behind me, Tamas's voice sang out. It was time to go.

10

EDITED TRANSCRIPT OF TAPE-RECORDED NOTES MADE BY MIHAI VLĂHUŢA

'It's late morning, December the fourth, and we've just stopped to eat. *Slănină* and bread, the usual muck. I'm sick of it by now, but I can't say anything to Tamas. He's returned to his old uncommunicative self, speaking only when spoken to, and then only in monosyllables.

'He's been behaving oddly all through our journey. From time to time, he pauses and tilts his head, as though listening for something. As far as I can tell, there is only the very great silence of the forest; but he listens all the same.

11

EDITED TRANSCRIPT OF TAPE-RECORDED NOTES MADE BY MIHAI VLĂHUŢA

'Another break. The snow's held off all day, but the temperature's still dropping. If the wolves don't get us, the cold will. We've got very few provisions, barely enough to see us through to tomorrow, and I'm growing worried in case something goes wrong. If we don't reach Castel Vlaicu by this evening, we'll be forced to spend the night out of doors.

'We've started climbing again. I'm recording this as we walk . . . Our path is flanked by these tall white trees. They're a pine of some sort. The forest . . .

[PAUSE.]

'Everywhere I look, it's just forest now. I can see a row or two of trees at the front, then it gets dark right after that.

'The sun's no longer over our heads, and it's growing dark long before sunset. I don't know what it is, but . . . well, the thing is, I'm getting really spooked out here. I keep touching the icon Father Gherasim gave me. Hope I'm not getting religion.

'I've been keeping a close lookout for wolves all day. A couple of times I've caught sight of a grey shape sliding between the trees,

131

and once or twice I've seen their eyes staring out from shadows. I haven't said a word about them to Tamas; but I've noticed his eyes straying to the forest when he thinks I'm not watching. Some of the trees seem very old, and their trunks are covered in ice.

'When we take a rest – which isn't often, he'll hardly let us stop – Tamas and Liliana sit away from me, talking in low voices. Tamas seems happy to talk with her, but he keeps his distance from me. Liliana says he's gone all deferential ever since he heard I'm a count; but, I don't know, I think it's more than that. I suppose . . . Actually, I think he's afraid of me. It doesn't make sense, does it?'

12

EXTRACT FROM THE JOURNAL OF
MIHAI VLĂHUŢA

4 December, late evening

We have reached our destination. I am sitting in my father's room, watching a fire flicker and die in the grate. There are no more logs. Outside, the wind and the darkness blot out everything. I feel more alone tonight, here in my father's home, than I have ever felt before.

It was an hour or so before sunset when we came on Castel Vlaicu at last. We had come to an open valley, wooded on all sides, with steep precipices walling it off in every direction except the one from which we had come. Ahead of us was a huddled group of low, mean-looking houses that straddled the path ahead. Near them, a frozen stream meandered across the valley floor.

'Vlaicu,' said Tamas, raising his hand and pointing. I followed his gaze, and as I did so, saw his finger lift until he was indicating, not the village, but something much higher up. Mist had come down from a high pass, and I had to strain to see what was the focus of his attention.

And then, as though brushed aside by his inarticulate gesture, a wall of mist vanished. It was as if the old photograph pasted in front of this journal had suddenly been enlarged and set down alive before me. High among mountains, in a cluster of snow-encrusted trees, the towers and cupolas and battlements and corbelled roofs of Castel Vlaicu hung suspended like a mirage. And there, directly in front of us, the path on which we walked continued, snaking its precipitous way up the mountainside to end at last at the castle's door. In a window high above the valley, a light burned. It was still daytime, but Castel Vlaicu seemed wreathed in a darkness of its own.

That was seven hours ago. Tamas brought us as far as the village, but would venture no further. Satu Vlaicu turned out to be even smaller and poorer than Silistraru. It was just a collection of hovels that had grown up higgledy-piggledy around the foot of the mountain. Wisps of grey smoke rose from low stone chimneys and drifted upwards as if to join the mist. Thin dogs ran through the single naked street, barking and whining at our unexpected approach. There was no church, not even a cross to mark the heart of the ragged place.

Tamas found a young boy feeding goats in a little shed at the entrance to the village. The air in the shed was fetid and rank with goat's urine, and the boy was dressed in rags that might not have been washed since he first put them on. Tamas gave his name and said where he had come from; the boy only stared as though human speech was alien to him. In the end, Tamas just repeated the name of the man he wanted to see, and finally the boy understood.

We were taken to a hovel at the other end of the village, and let into a dark, smoke-filled room whose air was little better than that of the goat-shed. The occupants were an old man, his wife, and a horde of what we took to be grandchildren. The man's name was Tibor, and he seemed to be some sort of village elder. Though they lived less than a summer day's journey apart, it seemed that he and Tamas had met only once or twice before. I gathered that there was little contact between Silistraru and Satu Vlaicu.

Tibor was a tough, wiry creature whom life had treated harshly. I could. not guess his age, but he looked eighty or more. Tamas told me later that he was not much more than fifty. The woman with him was his wife. She was younger than Tibor, but looked even older. I later learned that most of their children had died in childhood; the few that had survived had gone to the city – presumably Miercurea-Ciuc or Braşov – leaving behind their own brood. The youngsters seemed as unhealthy as their grandparents, and I imagine few of them will live to adulthood.

Tibor seemed not in the least surprised when told I was Count Vlăhuţa come to take up residence in my family home. My father and grandfather had already left Castel Vlaicu when he was born, though no doubt his own parents would have had memories of them.

'I saw a light in the castle as we were coming here,' I said. 'Does the caretaker live there?'

'There has always been someone in the castle,' he said. 'It is never empty.'

'Is there anyone else besides the caretaker?' I asked. 'I've no wish to throw anyone out. I'm sure there's room enough for everyone.'

He eyed me like someone troubled, as though I had said the wrong thing.

'There are two of them,' he said slowly. 'They live there night and day.'

They offered us a bed for the night, but neither Liliana nor I was keen to sleep or eat in that stinking hut. I asked if it wasn't possible for someone to take us to the castle before dark. They looked from one to the other, Tibor and his toothless wife, and for a while I thought they would say no or send us on to someone else.

'Very well,' said Tibor in the end. 'I'll take you. But we'll have to hurry. It will be dark soon.'

We said goodbye to Tamas. I gave him what I hoped was a generous reward. Without him, Liliana and I would certainly be dead now. He took the money reluctantly, but I could see it was welcome. As we turned to go, he took my hand in his and wished me well. I sensed there was something more he wanted to say, but at that moment Tibor came up to me and said there was no time to waste. We buttoned our coats again and followed him outside.

It is a steep climb from the village to the castle. The path is evidently little used, and in places it is quite broken away, making the climb more perilous than it need be. Even in spring or summer, it must present a formidable ascent; in winter it taxed us, exhausted as we were, to the limit. Building a proper path will be my first priority once I get to work here. Without a decent line of communications, Castel Vlaicu will remain isolated from the world.

Tibor hurried as along, urging us to climb faster by means of grunts and short, impatient gestures. In spite of his years, he himself was quite nimble-footed, and he remained ahead of us at every turn. From time to time, a bend in the path or a curtain of mist would block my view of the castle for a while. But it always returned, larger each time, perched on its steep crag like a great vulture with folded wings.

When we finally reached the top, I looked back for the first time over the darkening valley. The tiny village lay beneath our feet like a jumble of abandoned rocks, as much part of the natural landscape as a place of human habitation. My eyes ranged across the narrow valley, across the darkly wooded slopes that hemmed it in on every side, and finally came to rest again on the little houses directly below. This was where my family's serfs had once lived and died. Had they endured as much poverty as their descendants, I wondered, or had things been better then?

Set off at a little distance from the village itself, I saw a rectangular area, enclosed by a low wall. It took me a moment to comprehend what it was, then I saw that what I had taken for random stones in a field were, in fact, headstones arranged in irregular rows. But what most drew my attention were small flickering lights set among the graves. I turned to ask Tibor what they were for, but he had already gone ahead to the castle gate.

Walking the last short stretch to the castle, I looked up. There, set above the huge wooden door, was the same coat of arms that I had seen on our photograph album and in the library at Casă Feraru.

Tibor pulled a ring on a cord hanging beside the door. I could hear no bell, but he stood his ground confidently, awaiting a response. Minutes passed, and I grew anxious, knowing his eagerness to get back to the village before dark. The sky was already losing what light it had, and I knew he might decide to leave at any moment. It began to dawn on me that I had been extremely rash to insist on coming up here so late in the day.

'No one's coming,' said Liliana. I could sense my own anxiety reflected in her voice. 'I think we should go back down with Tibor. I'm not spending the night out here.'

Even as she spoke, however, I heard the sound of a door being raked across a stone floor, then footsteps crossing an open yard to the main gate.

The caretaker of Castel Vlaicu is a woman in her seventies called Elena. She is a gaunt, half-mad creature whose ravaged face and posture suggest a painful history that I cannot begin to guess at.

137

Compared to the runts we saw in Silistraru, or to Tibor and his wife, Elena is quite tall and very striking; at one time she may have been quite beautiful. But this is not what impresses one at first, for Elena is completely blind. Her eyes bear the traces of scars above and below, and I wonder if she was blinded as the result of an accident – or as a consequence of some violence committed on her.

It made absolutely no sense at first. How could a blind woman possibly be responsible for a place as vast as this, with all its passage-ways and staircases and empty apartments? The answer materialized moments later in the form of a companion, a man in his mid-forties who is, I gather, Elena's son. Of a husband, nothing has been said as yet, but I expect he's either dead or has abandoned her – not an uncommon occurrence in these parts, Liliana tells me.

The man's name is Costin. He's a well-built man, tall and strik-ingly handsome. I was favourably struck by him at first, but when I tried to speak to him, he grunted and shied away, as though he had not spoken to another human being in years. He appears surly and uncommunicative, and, as far as I can tell, he has spent his entire life shut up in this place with his blind mother. I've no idea how long she has been blind, or whether there was somebody else to look after her in Costin's early years, but no doubt all that will become clear in time.

Tibor mumbled an incoherent explanation of our presence, told us the woman's name, then the man's, and made his getaway as fast as his spindly legs would carry him. He didn't even hang round to be paid for his trouble. When I last saw him, his little figure was skit-tering down the path, hurrying to get back before twilight turned to night.

Liliana explained who we were and what we were doing there in considerably greater detail than Tibor had been able to muster. Elena listened impassively, while Costin glared at us without betraying the least sign that he understood a word of what was said. It's not that he's retarded in any way, merely that he seems totally unfamiliar with life outside the castle.

No letter had arrived, though I doubted that Costin could have read it anyway. I realized we had planned things very badly. The castle may by rights belong to me, but for the moment it is Elena's and Costin's home, and it wouldn't be surprising if they were put out to have us arrive unannounced on their doorstep.

'I'm sorry,' I said, making my apologies far too late. 'We should have made sure you knew we were coming.'

She brushed off my apologies, leaving me with the feeling that I was her guest and she a magnanimous hostess in whose home I would be permitted to stay for a few nights. We followed them into the castle through a low doorway in the south wall, and from there through a series of bare, winding corridors to what I already think of as their lair. Costin carried a heavy oil lamp that gave off as many fumes as it did light.

They had created a space for themselves out of three or four rooms on the first floor. It was from the window of one of these rooms that I had seen the light earlier, Costin's one concession to his own needs in the world of sight. Otherwise, their apartment was dark, as though it and the castle for the most part echoed Elena's darkness. I noticed candles here and there, unlit, set there, no doubt, for Costin's occasional use. A fire burned in the grate in the largest room, but the main source of warmth was the thick clothes Elena and Costin wore on their bodies.

Elena absented herself for a time. We sat with the silent Costin, huddled near the fire, scarcely daring to break the wider silence of Castel Vlaicu. I felt out of place. I had no sense of kinship with this cold, stark monument, no feeling that I belonged here, that an ancient link existed between my blood and these grey stones.

Elena returned with two plates of food, bowls of bean soup with noodles, which we devoured eagerly, Costin watching us all the time with an incurious gaze. I wondered where their food came from, and for the first time considered the problem of how Liliana and I were to obtain provisions. Obviously we could hardly depend on Elena's own doubtless meagre supply; but as winter settled more heavily on the countryside, stocks of food would presumably be rationed.

I wondered too how she and Costin lived. Who exactly paid them to act as caretakers at Castel Vlaicu? Were they state functionaries of some kind, left here to ensure the castle did not become too derelict, while a faceless committee in Bucharest or Cluj-Napoca dreamed up some use for it? Or were they just villagers who preferred to live apart from their families? Elena does not have a local accent, which suggests she may have been sent out originally from the capital; but she could just as easily have married a villager (a soldier, perhaps) and settled here with him.

I mean to find out all I can as soon as I can raise the topic without seeming rude. I feel that my position here is still anomalous. Neither she nor her son can read my papers, and I have no other means of proving my identity. Whatever the legal position, Liliana and I are here on sufferance.

When we had eaten, Elena ordered Costin to busy himself making a room ready for us. I did not enter into explanations about the nature of my relationship to Liliana. That, after all, is our business. Elena and Costin are caretakers here, they have no other status, and they have no right to question my morals or behaviour.

I asked if my father's old room would be suitable, and Elena smiled and said, yes, it would. Later, I mean to have a room set up especially for us, but in the meantime this will do, and it will create a sense of continuity.

With Costin out of the way, Elena offered to show us a little of the castle. I almost turned her offer down, saying that I would prefer to see the place by daylight, but awkwardness held me back: after all, it made no difference to her what time of day or night it was.

'There's a lamp next to the fire,' she said. 'You'd best bring it with you.' Her voice is curiously deep, almost like a man's, and resonant. It has the quality of a voice that is seldom used. I don't suppose she and Costin find much to talk about.

We set off after her, astonished at the ease with which she got around. She used a stick sparingly, seeming to know the twists and turns of the castle's innumerable passages as though a map had been implanted in her brain.

Everywhere, shadows went ahead of us, everywhere they followed us so closely I would look round, expecting small, scuttling footsteps. But the only footsteps there were our own, amplified by the stone walls and empty stretches of corridors or landings. We walked through a silence that seemed as old as the forests or the mountains ringing us about. I have never been so conscious of my own breathing or my heartbeat, never so aware that I am alive. We were the only living things in a vast maze of stone and shadows.

Nothing had been changed. Not in years, perhaps not in centuries. The light would come to rest on a strange assortment of trophies and heirlooms – my inheritance snatched out of the shadows for brief moments. Portraits with staring eyes, battledress, plumed helmets, lances, muskets, halberds, the heads of bears and wolves and deer, shields with the Vlăhuţa crest – stern reminders of my ancestors' military careers. Through briefly opened doors we would catch sight of a forgotten past: chairs and tables sheeted in dust, clocks frozen in time, the marble heads of ancient heroes looped with cobwebs. Once or twice, we saw our own faces reflected back at us from dusty mirrors, surreal, pallid, and afraid in the preternatural glow of the smoky lamp.

It all still seems unreal, and as incoherent as a dream. No sequence, no pattern, no reason behind anything, just images out of nightmare, shuffled and presented to our gaze like slides on a flickering screen. Liliana walked beside me, clutching my hand in hers, voiceless and afraid. Castel Vlaicu is a dark and disturbing place whose silences tear at the mind, as though something is, after all, being said or whispered in there among the shadows, as though a barely heard voice is speaking.

I had thought that coming here would bring me some sort of peace, that it would loosen all the knots of discontent and confusion life has tied in me. Now that I am here, I am less sure. I'm tired, of course, and in need of sleep, but my mind is too busy to allow me rest. I watch the firelight dancing on the walls, making and unmaking grotesque phantom shapes against the blurred tapestries that surround the room. Liliana sleeps on the double bed, as far from me as her dreams will take her.

My window looks out across the valley. I'm writing this at a little desk set under it, and if I lift my eyes I can look down into the darkness. Below me, beside the village, the tiny lights are still twinkling in the graveyard.

13

LETTER FROM MRS ROSEMARY FERARU TO MICHAEL FERARU (MIHAI VLĂHUŢA)

The Queen Marie Guest House
York Villas
Harrogate
Yorkshire

4 December

My Dear Michael,

Darling, did you get my last letter, the one I sent after the telegram?
I think I may have sent it to your hotel by mistake, only I've been so
flustered recently, I haven't been able to think straight, in fact my
brain's all quite muddled, and I hardly know what I'm doing at times.
Brenda's a tremendous help, I don't know what I'd do without her,
I really don't, and I hope she doesn't lose her head completely over
young Peter, it wouldn't work out, and I'd be at a complete loss if
she went off somewhere, as young people are in the habit of doing
nowadays. You'd know all about that, of course, darling, you've done
plenty of going off in your time. Not that I hold it against you or

anything, though I would like to have seen more of you in recent years. Still, I suppose you have your own life to lead and important things to be getting on with, orphanages and suchlike, and I'm only your old mother after all.

But, darling, I so hope you got my letter, because I explained in it why you shouldn't go to your old family home, as I wrote in my telegram. You'll just have to get in touch, and I'll repeat everything I know, and if there's anything you don't understand, I'll explain it. The main thing is not going there, not under any circumstances.

Darling, I have some very bad news, which I know will upset you, in fact, it quite shocked me to hear it, though I'd never met the man himself. Your old headmaster, Arthur Drewe, died of a heart attack on the twenty-ninth of last month. He was only sixty-three, I believe – well, that's young nowadays, isn't it? And you used to say he was such an active man, and kind to the boys. I explained to the woman who rang that you were hard to get hold of, though I gave her your address. She said she'd write, but I thought I might as well mention it myself.

Darling, you mustn't upset yourself over anything I said in that letter. It's all true, I do assure you, I wouldn't make a fuss like that over nothing, you know me better than that. If you'd only drop a line or two, or better still, ring so I can hear your voice and know you're all right.

Your anxious mother.

144

14

Edited transcript of tape-recorded notes made by Mihai Vlăhuţa

'It's late morning . . . about . . . let's see . . . eleven on the fifth of December. There's been light seeping through my windows for several hours, but I've managed to sleep on regardless: my exhaustion's caught up with me at last. All the same, I don't feel in the least refreshed. My legs are aching like billy-o, and my head feels as though it's been stuffed with boiled rice, like a giant pepper. I've got a fucking awful headache, and about as much hope of finding aspirin as coming across a fridge full of caviar.

'There's . . . something here . . . something I don't want to put in the journal. It was . . .

[LONG PAUSE.]

'I had dreams all night. Bad dreams, I don't . . . I can't remember much about them now, but they've left their mood in me. It won't be easy to shake it off. It's a . . . mood of despair more than anything. I . . .

'In one of the dreams I saw a very old man with long white hair. He was standing next to an open grave and. . .

[PAUSE.]

145

'And staring hard at me. He frightened the hell out of me.

'And then, there was another one. There was a blind woman, and she was following me down a stone corridor.

In the distance someone was thumping on a great door. At least, for some reason I thought it was a door. I can still hear the booming inside my head.'

15

EXTRACT FROM THE JOURNAL OF
MIHAI VLĂHUȚA

5 December

Our bedroom is on the floor above the caretakers' apartment. It must have been decorated last in the eighteen hundreds. If my father did indeed live here, he must have taken all his belongings with him, for I can see nothing that might have been his. The chamber is dominated by a vast four-poster bed complete with heavy brocaded hangings that look as though they haven't been washed since they were first put up. I scarcely dare ask for them to be taken down and cleaned, for fear they'll just turn to dust. The same goes for most of the other furnishings. The curtains at the window are in the same condition as those round the bed, and the fabric on most of the chairs has rotted badly.

I fear the whole castle is in the same state. During last night's short excursion I saw traces of decay at almost every turn. I'll be able to see round properly today and form some sort of impression about what has to be done. But it looks as though Castel Vlaicu has just been left to rot since it was taken from my family. I'd expected something a little different, though I don't know what exactly. A state-run home for elderly peasants, or a hunting-lodge for government apparatchiks: anything but this.

As things stand, it's likely to be impossibly expensive to convert the whole place into an orphanage. Charitable donations will only go so far, and donors want to see smiling faces and bonny babies in months, not years. In any case, I'm not sure an orphanage would be practicable here. The weather and the isolation in winter alone would be almost insuperable problems.

Liliana's idea of turning the place into an hotel seems to have more merit than I thought at first. If I could get financial backing for the renovation, we could turn the drawbacks into advantages and be up and running in a couple of years. It would mean lucrative work for local people. The main thing is that the castle could be preserved much as it is now, but vastly improved. I don't think it would be an impossible task to get it looking much as it did in my grandfather's day.

Costin's just come to tell me there's breakfast if I want it. He says Liliana's there already, waiting for me.

16

EXTRACT FROM THE JOURNAL OF
MIHAI VLĂHUȚA

5 December, late afternoon

It will be sunset again soon. I have found a small sitting room and am trying to make it hospitable. It will be my base from which to explore the rest of the castle. Costin has been fetching and carrying for me since this morning, and by the looks of it, it's the first real work he's done in years. I've done my fair share as well, of course, but Elena seemed eager for him to do as much of the lifting and moving as possible. She seems to think it will do him good. He's been getting idle, she says, with no one to work for, and now I'm here she believes it will ginger him up. He doesn't appear to share her opinion, but I'm grateful to have him all the same. I couldn't dream of knocking this place into shape without help.

Anyway, I now have a decent inlaid table to serve as a desk, and some chairs, including the one I'm sitting on at this moment, a rather elegant piece of furniture that's upholstered in good leather, which Costin has polished until it looks fit for a palace. I've had all manner of junk cleared out, and as I come across other decent bits and pieces,

I'll have them brought here. There's a fireplace, and no shortage of logs. I thought the chimney might be blocked after all these years, but it draws perfectly, and I have a magnificent blaze that makes me think of roasting chestnuts and Christmas carols.

Liliana has spent most of the day in her own discovery, the castle library, which is a corridor or so from here. She has a fire going in there as well, and when I last saw her she was sitting with Elena, talking and going through the books. Quite a few of them have been damaged, but the majority seem to have survived, as far as it's possible to tell from a random check.

The library must have been one of the finest rooms in the castle. It's on two levels, with a broad gallery that stretches round three walls. Downstairs, there's a main reading room, with smaller shelf-lined rooms leading off it at one end. The shelves are high, with ladders attached to metal rails, all rusted now and difficult to move. I'd guess that the room was laid out as far back as the sixteenth century, with changes and additions down the years.

At the moment, it's a gloomy room. The windows, which are high up, haven't been cleaned in decades, and very little light manages to creep through. There are sconces for candles everywhere, carefully designed to reduce the risk of fire, but it will take some time to get even those in working order. Liliana has arranged a reading table for herself in front of a window, and has a little lamp that gives sufficient light to work by for an hour or two at a time.

I found her there a little while ago, working alone among the shadows, and when I kissed her gently, she responded with a passion that surprised me. We did not make love last night, we were both much too tired; but our exhaustion seems to have worn off already, and in its place I can sense the beginnings of a curious, primitive energy that makes our need for one another almost painful.

Whether from sentiment or wit, Liliana has put the old doll on top of the desk, giving the room a rather homely feel. She seems content enough to work in there, though, and I've encouraged her in the hope she may find family papers. I am growing desperate for knowledge of my antecedents and myself.

In one respect, I have learned a little more today about my ancestors. The room I have made my study contains portraits of about a dozen male members of the family, mainly from the eighteenth and nineteenth centuries. They are stylized paintings, mostly in oils, with a couple of pastels by Liotard, done in the 1740s.

They are all quite alien to me, tall, bearded *boyars* in their fur-lined robes, beneath which they wear Turkish silks and Persian brocades. On their heads, they wear the most extraordinary fur hats with coloured plumes, four or five feet high, and I try to imagine them as they must have looked to the peasants down in the village, giants nine and ten foot tall, with the power of life or death. Their faces are arrogant and cruel, and I think they belong, not just to a different age, but to another world entirely. And yet these are my ancestors, their blood runs in my veins. Their blood, and what else besides?

17

LETTER FROM SOPHIE WANDLESS TO
MIHAI VLĂHUȚA

90 Mill Road
Cambridge

5 December

Darling,

I'm going frantic trying to get hold of you. Your mother says you may have gone off to the castle already, but I can't believe that. I spoke to someone in the Foreign Office yesterday, who said travel in that region had come to a complete standstill on account of the weather, and that things weren't likely to improve now until spring. So I imagine you're still in Bucharest, or at worst in another town. Why didn't you stay in your hotel? I could at least get hold of you there, or leave a message.

Your mother sounded very distressed when I spoke to her, and I think I may try to get a day or two to go up to Harrogate, just to see she's all right. I couldn't get much sense out of her on the phone, other than something about the castle, that it's dangerous, and that you shouldn't go there. I told her you couldn't possibly have gone there, that, even if you'd left, you'd never have made it through the Carpathians, and that seemed to calm her down quite a bit. All the same, I'm a little worried about her, and I think you should give her a ring the moment you get this letter.

I take it you've heard of Arthur Drewe. He was found dead in his bedroom at the Headmaster's House on the morning of the twenty-ninth. Heart failure, or so they're saying; but I've heard there may be more to it than that. Jean wasn't there at the time, she'd gone to London with Jack Matthews's parents. Christ, Michael, I wonder if you know about any of this. Jack Matthews was killed on the twenty-seventh, knocked down by a hit-and-run driver as he was leaving the Arts Theatre. He'd been to a guitar recital with a couple of other lads; they were hurt, but not too badly.

Then, two days later, the housekeeper found old Drewe stone cold in bed. There's a rumour going round the school that he died of fright. I'd put that down as a schoolboy fantasy if it weren't for the fact I heard it from Alan Hardiman. Apparently, there was to have been an inquest, but it's been called off and the whole business hushed up on account of some diaries Drewe left behind. I scent a whiff of a sex scandal, except that – well, it doesn't have quite that feel about it. And old Drewe was hardly the type. Mind you, Jean was away at the time. God, it seems really sordid.

Look, I haven't heard from you since the middle of November. No doubt you and your nubile little lawyer friend are having a lovely time, but I'd like a little attention now and then, if I may. And just so you remember what you're missing, I'm writing this in bed, wearing nothing but the Lejaby bra and pants you bought me last Christmas. Remember? The ones with the little lace panel in front and the bows at the side. Of course, if I were to take them off . . .

> Sweet dreams,
> Sophie

18

EXTRACT FROM THE JOURNAL OF
MIHAI VLĂHUŢA

7 December

The days pass now without variety, soft and silent, and as dull as lead. We go about our separate tasks within the castle, and meet again for meals, or sit about a fire and talk of what we plan. It has snowed heavily, twice in two days, and Costin says we are quite cut off now, even from the village.

I was worried at first about food, but Elena has enough in her larder to last us to spring and the thaw, if need be. It's not the best of fare by any means, but it will keep us alive. I offered her money for our share, but she refused it, and I can see now how little point there was in the offer. Where would she go with money, what would she spend it on? Instead, I've promised to restock the larder when spring comes. I'll do better than that, of course – I'll have provisions brought in from Bucharest, and next winter we'll live like kings.

In my explorations so far, I have found no sign of the family chapel. I had expectations of a glorious Orthodox interior, filled with icons and precious stones. But Elena says there is no chapel, that there never was one. I find that hard to believe. Every noble family had its chapel. There is no church in Satu Vlaicu, so there must have been one up here for the family. I suggested to Elena that the chapel might have been shut down when the Communists took over, but she shook her head and said no chapel had ever been built.

Beyond my window, the snow drifts down like a curse. It is thick and coarse, and it blots out everything outside the castle. The valley, the village, the entire world might have been wiped out for all I know. England is so far away, I scarcely dare think of it. Or, for that matter, of Sophie. She must be worried sick, but I tell myself there's nothing I can do, there's no way I can get a message out to her or anyone else.

Even if I could, what message would I send? Liliana shares my bed every night now, hot and clinging like an odalisque, and throughout the day images of her naked body accompany me like phantoms of the night before. I do not think I could, in all honesty, write to Sophie now with any conviction of love or need. We were almost man and wife, we shared our lives for four years, and we dreamed of a future together. But if I think of that time now, I see us both as pale, dim creatures, wraiths with little substance living lives without passion.

It is very different with Liliana. We make love as though possessed, as though something in each of us sought to devour the other. I would caress her each and every minute of the clay if I could. Sophie was demure, almost passive in bed, taking her pleasure carefully, and returning it in small, measured doses, but Liliana is like the fire I can hear behind me as I write, raging, consumed by its own heat.

I will write to Sophie in the spring and tell her everything, if she does not guess already. Perhaps she's sleeping with Derek Hignett by now. No heat or passion there. They're well suited.

* * *

Elena comes to my sitting room for an hour every afternoon. She seems shy of me, though whether that is because I am a foreigner, or a man, or a count, I cannot tell. I've been trying to find out about her and her son, and the history of Castel Vlaicu since it was taken over by the state. She tells me very little, but I shall set Liliana to prise more out of her in time.

The castle, she says, remains exactly as it was when the notice of requisition arrived. Not a stick of furniture, not a book, not the tiniest ornament has ever been removed. Dust and damp have been the enemies here, not ideologues or bureaucrats. She was twenty-seven at the time, and already living in the castle.

'Were you a servant?' I asked.

She shook her head.

'Not exactly,' she said, her eyes fixed unseeingly on a spot a little to my left.

'What then? A governess?'

She just shook her head and went to another subject. Her reticence irritates me, but Liliana says I shall get nowhere if I show impatience or, worse still, anger, so I stay calm and talk about what there is to be done here.

Costin was born not long after the takeover, so I guess his father must have been either a man from the village, or one of the castle staff.

'What happened to the staff?' I asked. 'Did they have anywhere to go?'

She shrugged.

'They were all local people,' she said. 'They went back to their families. To Satu Vlaicu, most of them.'

'Are any of them still there?' I asked.

157

She shook her head.

'All dead now,' she said in a sad, drained voice. Her eyes wandered, seeing nothing, to here and there. I wondered what she saw.

'Have you always been blind?' I asked. She seemed so confident in her movements, and yet many of her memories implied a time when she had been able to see.

'Not always,' she said, and plunged off to another topic.

19

EXTRACT FROM THE JOURNAL OF MIHAI VLĂHUȚA

8 December

Something curious happened today. Now that my sitting room-cum-study has been set in a little order, I've been taking the opportunity to explore the castle more thoroughly. It is a maze of passageways and stairs, with as few windows to the outside as could be contrived without consigning the inhabitants to utter darkness. Castel Vlaicu is a fortress rather than a ducal palace, and its towers and battlements were built for defence, not ornament. The various wings combine to create a jigsaw whose overall pattern – if there is one – is still not apparent to me. Stone gives way to wood, and wood again to stone, corridors end abruptly against walls, doors open onto gloomy court-yards that seem to have no purpose. In one there is a fountain long dried up, in another the trunk of a tree, withered many years ago.

This morning after breakfast, I decided to explore the north wing, a vast crypt of a place that is, by all appearances, the oldest part of the castle. It is built entirely of stone, with heavy lintels above the doors, and huge flagstones for paving in the corridors. I felt quite uneasy to be there alone, with no company but the sound of my own footsteps ringing on the flags. There are niches in the walls, where candles or torches must have burned at one time. But there are none there now, and the darkness is almost too thick for my tiny lamp to dispel.

At one end, the main corridor leads into a squat tower. There are no proper rooms in the upper levels, only a series of white-painted circular chambers devoid of furniture or decoration. The walls are still white, but marred by patches of mould and damp. The rooms may at one time have been used for storage, or even to quarter animals in time of siege. The same spiral staircase that gives access to these storeys also descends some thirty feet or more below ground level.

I wondered what might be down there. Ever since starting my explorations, I have been hoping to find the wine cellar, if there is one. Should I come to open Hotel Vlaicu, what could be more enticing than a well-stocked cellar bulging with pre-war vintages? My father used to talk of the wines he enjoyed as a boy: French wines of every kind, Tokai from Hungary, and the best Romanian varieties, above all the Crown wines grown on the royal estates. Cotnari, Odobeşti, Drăgăşani, and other names I forget.

As I climbed down, however, all thoughts of wine were driven from my mind by the atmosphere of that dark and musty stairwell. If Castel Vlaicu is a gloomy and cheerless place, then the heart of that gloom is there, in that silent tower. The further down I went, the deeper grew my sense of uneasiness and foreboding, as if I might at any moment encounter a very great evil. I almost turned back more than once, wishing fervently I had not gone there alone, yet unwilling to admit to myself that I could so easily be scared off. I remembered my experience in Casă Feraru, that abandoned room, the man's voice whispering, the baby's sudden cry.

When I reached the bottom of the stairs, I saw in front of me a heavy wooden door set with enormous iron hinges and a stout lock. By now, I was tempted to return and come back later, if at all, with someone else. But some last shred of courage or stubbornness held me there. I reached out for the handle and tried to turn it. I will freely admit that I was almost relieved when it would not budge. The door was firmly locked, and I did not have a key.

By the time if got back to the body of the castle, I'd calmed down a great deal, and was already dismissing my nervousness of minutes earlier as a result of stress and isolation. My thoughts were already returning to a wine list crammed with exotic vintages and prices with plenty of noughts on the end.

I found Elena alone in her apartment, preparing our midday meal. She's not much of a cook, but I have to admire the skill with which she does it all, her hands moving with practised exactitude through every movement, so that nothing spills or is lost. Everything has its place, each bowl and plate and cup is set a prescribed distance from the next, nothing is left to chance.

She heard me coming long before I reached her. Her hearing is remarkably sensitive. Sometimes she seems to hear things neither Liliana nor I are conscious of.

'Elena,' I said, 'I've just been to the tower in the north wing. There's a door at the bottom of the stairs, but it's locked. You don't have the key, do you?'

She had half turned in order to present her face to me. In her hand she held a glass in which she had been stirring oil. As I spoke, her face altered and the glass dropped from her hand, shattering on the stone floor. Flustered, she bent down and scrabbled among the fragments, cutting herself.

'No,' I said, grabbing her arm and pulling her upright. 'Leave that to me.'

I took her hand and held it to the light. One finger was bleeding badly.

'You've hurt yourself,' I said. 'Let me see if there's any glass in it.'

I managed to get her into another room. She told me where to find some strips of cloth that were used for bandages, and I bound her finger.

'I'm sorry I startled you,' I said.

'It's not your fault, sir. I heard you coming.'

'Was it something I said?'

She seemed to get flustered again.

'What is it? Is it something to do with the tower?'

She shook her head.

'It's nothing. I was careless.'

'What's down there? I thought a wine cellar or something like that.'

Again a vehement shake of the head. Her eyes fluttered in their sockets, as though struggling to escape me.

'No wine cellar. The wine cellar is beneath this part. I'll ask Costin to take you there.'

'And the door at the bottom of the tower? Is there a key?'

Her head did not move. She held it in a very great stillness. Her eyes were fixed ahead of her, as though staring at something or someone behind me. I was almost prompted to look round, but I forced myself to use sense. The woman is blind, she cannot see.

'No,' she said, pulling herself together, almost like someone who has been daydreaming and brings herself back to focus. 'There's no key.'

'Are you quite sure?' I asked. 'Have you never been down there?'

She hesitated, and I knew she was lying when she answered.

'No,' she said, 'never.'

'But surely you know what's there.'

She shook her head, and I thought for the first time she seemed tired – tired and old and trying to shake herself free of something. She grew still again, and her eyes seemed to return to the spot behind my shoulder, on which they had been fixed before.

I said no more. When I had finished bandaging Elena's wounded finger, I went out and cleared away the shards of broken glass. She waited in her darkness without moving, until I returned and told her the floor was safe to walk on once more.

20

Extract from the Journal of Mihai Vlăhuţa

8 December, evening

Costin took me to the wine cellar this afternoon. It's in a very poor state. The bottles are thick with cobwebs, and no attempt has been made to control the temperature, with the result that the couple of bottles I opened had turned vinegary and were quite undrinkable. I fear the rest may be the same or worse. Perhaps I'll just steam off the labels and stick them on some bottles of local table wine. A spot of dust, a few cobwebs, and half the guests won't know the difference.

While we were there, I tried to pump him about the door at the foot of the tower, but without success. He just backed off into his shell, grunted, shook his head, and ignored my questions. All the same, I can tell that, like his mother, he knows something.

I spoke to Liliana about it an hour or so ago, but she can hazard no better guess than I. She has promised to help me find a key. We are both confident that one exists.

21

LETTER FROM SOPHIE WANDLESS TO
MIHAI VLĂHUȚA

90 Mill Road
Cambridge

9 December

Michael,

For God's sake, ring or something. Your mother's worried sick, and so am I. It's weeks since either of us heard from you, you're not at your hotel, you don't answer letters sent to your apartment, Liliana Popescu or whatever her name is isn't in the phone book, and we don't know if you're in Bucharest or stuck in some hole in the mountains or ill or dead or what!

I've spoken with your mother, and she's convinced me something *is* wrong out there. She's shown me some papers, mostly letters written to your grandfather, that refer to certain events in your family history, things that have happened mainly at Vlaicu Castle (I hope that's the right spelling). It's all very vague, I admit, since the various people who wrote to your grandfather took it for granted he knew what they

165

were speaking about. The letters are signed, but the signatures are all unreadable, and your mother has no idea of their authorship. All she knows is that they speak more than once of people dying at the castle, and of 'dark secrets' that can never be told. I know it sounds almost farcical, but, believe me, Michael, these letters weren't written for anybody's amusement.

What makes all this worse for your mother is that she has dreams of your father almost every night now, and she's convinced he's trying to get through to her, to warn her about some danger facing you. I've done my best to play this down, but she won't be talked out of it, and I've got to admit she's done a pretty good job of spooking me. If we could just *talk*, it would make all this easier to cope with.

To cap it all, there's been a further tragedy at King William's. I had a call yesterday from Percy Lyall, who's been appointed acting head until the board of governors can decide on Drewe's successor. They'll have to advertise, so it may take till the end of next term. Anyway, Percy heard I'd been asking after Jean, and he just rang to let me know how things are with her.

The fact is, she's not coping very well. She says she's been hearing voices saying the most evil things, and Percy thinks she may be headed for a breakdown. This would be bad enough, but I'm afraid there's worse. Another boy was killed, young Nigel Blake. I know you were fond of him. They found him at the foot of Bodley Stairs: it looks as though he must have slipped and fallen from the top, breaking his neck, though nobody knows what he was doing there. It's doubly ironic because he was due to take over responsibility for the Romanian orphanage project following Jack Matthews's death. You'd think the whole thing was jinxed. Some of the staff are thinking of calling it off. It's not too late, and I told him you'd be more relieved than sorry if they did.

If I don't hear from you by next week, I'm coming out.

XXXXXXXXX
Sophie

22

EXTRACT FROM THE JOURNAL OF
MIHAI VLĂHUŢA

12 December

As the days pass, Castel Vlaicu impresses itself ever more deeply on my mind and senses, even in my dreams. I wander through its passages like a dog prowling the streets of a dead city, in search of light or warmth or habitation, and finding none.

The snow has eased off, and the horizon is composed of mountain and forest once more. At night, the lights flicker in the graveyard again. By day, the forest remains dark, a primeval place into which no one ventures, from which no one comes. There is no sun. I am afraid.

What do I fear? Nothing. I have seen nothing, heard nothing. The old man comes to me in my dreams, that is all. He stares at me, then he goes, that is all. When he walks away, there is a sound of singing somewhere, I cannot tell where, that is all. But I am afraid. I spend each day now with a mounting sense of dread, as if this place contains something evil, something that has been asleep but is now coming slowly awake.

23

NOTES FROM LILIANA POPESCU'S 'MICHAEL FERARU/MIHAI VLĂHUȚA' FILE (UNDATED)

Mihai's getting jumpy. I'm not sure how much he knows, he won't speak to me about it, but he's starting to show signs of anxiety. Has he seen something?

The old woman knows more than she's telling. Mihai seems completely taken in by her. He hasn't noticed her accent, or, if he has, he doesn't know what to make of it. I've tried questioning her, but she steers me on to something else. Yesterday, she let slip that she'd lived in Bucharest. I'd already guessed that from the accent, of course. But it's a lot more than that, it's class as well. What's a woman like her doing in a place like this, working as a caretaker? A mere irony of the revolution? Or something more?

The library is astonishing. I'm way out of my depth, of course, but you don't have to know much about this sort of thing to see just how rare some of the volumes are, and what a fine collection it must have been at one time. The destruction is tragic – worse than that, criminal. Letting books like these go to rot is such a waste. Of course, Elena doesn't read and Costin can't, so they haven't given the library a moment's thought. They leave me in here for most of the day, which suits me fine.

I'm reading all I can about the Vlăhuţas. What I've read so far confirms everything I knew before, but has added very few details. I understand now why Mihai was not allowed entry to the church at Silistraru, and why they light candles in the cemetery below at night. But I still do not know when it began, or why, or whether there will ever be an end.

Mihai's the most naive man I have ever come across. Are all Englishmen like him? He thinks I love him, when I simply like sleeping with him. I want him to go back to his woman in Cambridge when he leaves in the spring, but he's already talking about taking me home with him. What Mihai needs is a wife, someone to have his babies and darn his socks and cook his fish and chips, or whatever it is good English wives do; not a hard-nosed Romanian bitch like me, who wants neither babies nor home comforts, but enough money to make a go of it as a lawyer back in Bucharest. Assuming, of course, that I ever see the place again.

I heard the whispering again last night. Mihai seemed to hear nothing, or pretended that he did not. Sometimes I see Elena move her head when we talk, as though she hears something I do not. Her hearing is more acute than mine, of course. But I think the whispering is more than my imagination, and that it is the whispering she hears.

24

EXTRACT FROM THE JOURNAL OF MIHAI VLĂHUŢA

13 December

We are not alone in the castle. Early this morning, while Liliana was still asleep, I stepped into the passage on my way to the bathroom. I saw a man standing at the end of the corridor, caught in a patch of dawn light where it fell transversely through a high, tilted window. I was still half asleep, for I had risen earlier than usual, but I saw him clearly enough – a young man in a long black coat, his hair grown over his ears, his beard dark and neatly trimmed. He was staring in my direction, as though startled to see me there.

I was flummoxed at first, not knowing what to do or say. For all the world, I could not begin to guess where he had come from or what he might be doing in that corridor at that hour. I opened my mouth to say something, but he turned his back abruptly, and a moment later he had slipped round the corner. I followed him, but by the time I reached the bend, he had gone completely. I carried on in that direction for a little while, but it was soon dark, and my oil lamp showed no one in the passage ahead.

The man seemed much younger than Costin, in his mid-twenties or thereabouts, and his whole appearance was very distinctive, so I was sure I had not mistaken Costin for someone unknown. Later, when Liliana was awake, I told her what I had seen. Her reaction astonished me.

'Tell me what he looked like,' she asked.

Her face had turned quite pale, and at first I thought she must be thinking I'd seen a ghost or something of that sort. I remembered my unpleasant experience that day at Casă Feraru, and started to think all sorts of things myself.

As I described the young man to Liliana, her eyes widened, as though all I said confirmed what she was already thinking. But it was not ghosts she was thinking of. She asked a few more questions, then sat down on the edge of the bed, looking quite defeated.

'It must be Nicu,' she said. 'He must have followed me here.'

'Nicu? Who's he?'

She explained, in faltering words, like someone drugged. An old boyfriend, her lover from time to time, their scheme to get Nicu involved in my hotel project, my perceived usefulness. It all poured out of her, each confession a slap in the face, until I asked her to stop.

I'm angry, and hurt, and disappointed, and I lost no time in telling Liliana. She made no apologies, just accused me of being more English than Romanian, and unable to understand the pressures they live under, the false morality they have created for themselves, like insects mimicking affection.

We spent several hours after that prowling the corridors with lamps in hand, calling her friend's name. She did the calling, of course, in order not to frighten him. She has no idea how he may have got into the castle. When questioned, both Elena and Costin denied that anyone had come. It would have been impossible, they said, the roads are impassable by now, no one could possibly get through.

No one answered, and we gave up in the end. Liliana's confident we'll flush him out in the end. He has to eat, and without some sort of heat, he risks freezing to death.

25

EXTRACT FROM THE JOURNAL OF MIHAI VLĂHUȚA

13 December, early evening

I'm beginning to wonder if I wasn't dreaming this morning. I went outside this afternoon and examined the track that leads up to the castle. It's the only approach: there is thick forest on all other sides, and above the castle. No one can get to Castel Vlaicu other than through the village. The path is an even expanse of deep snow. I saw nothing on it, not even the tracks of a bird.

I have told Liliana I want to sleep alone from now on. Costin made up a bed for her in the room she had the first night we were here. He expressed no surprise or curiosity. Elena came afterwards to say she was sorry we had quarrelled, and to ask Liliana if she would be all right on her own.

'I'll be all right,' Liliana told her.

'If you need me, you know where I am,' Elena said, then left in a hurry. There seems to be something between them, a secret, something they understand but I don't. Liliana is anxious. I'm almost tempted to tell her to stay after all, but I still feel betrayed and used. In time, perhaps. We have all winter to get through, it would be madness to become enemies now.

26

EXTRACT FROM THE JOURNAL OF
MIHAI VLĂHUŢA

14 December

I heard the wolves again last night, several at once, then a single wolf whose howling seemed to go on forever. They sounded restless, as though hunger or cold were driving them to acts of desperation. I went to the window several times and looked for them in the snow. There was a full moon, but I could see nothing. I think they must be in the forest at the rear of the castle. Their voices sounded close. Each time I looked out, I saw lights in the cemetery. Do the villagers visit the graves by night, I wonder? If so, what is it they are frightened of?

I mentioned the wolves to Elena. She muttered something I did not understand and left the room.

27

FROM A SHORT MANUSCRIPT HISTORY OF THE
VLĂHUŢA FAMILY BY FATHER ANGHEL DE LA
AFUMAŢI, CONTAINED IN A BOUND COLLECTION
ENTITLED *Documente privitoare la Barbu Vlăhuţa
(1757),* AND DISCOVERED BY LILIANA POPESCU IN
THE LIBRARY AT CASTEL VLAICU

IT IS SAID THAT the first of this family to cheat death
was Matei Vlăhuţa, whose father, Iordache, fought
the Turks at Kossovo with John Hunyadi, and was
the builder of the tower at Vlaicu, about which the
castle was subsequently erected. There was in those
days a party of discontents who raised the banner of
rebellion with the slogan

*Universitas regnicolarum Hungarorum et
Valachorum in his partibus Transilvaniae*

Which motto meant, for all its wordiness, no more
than that the base should rule in place of the noble,

and that the cesspit should be raised above the palace – a contemptible philosophy which, even in these days, has been much revived, to the little credit of our age or the repute of Christian wisdom. Matei discreetly entered into a compact with the Hungarian nobility of the region, and, with his father's reputation going ahead of him, rendered illustrious service to the *voivode*. In the year 1454, he put down a rising in the Harghita with such ruthlessness and the shedding of such quantities of peasant blood that none there has dared rebel since. By way of reward he was given lands and made count of Vlaicu, himself and his descendants, in perpetuity. Though a Vlach, he rose to eminence and proved himself a loyal vassal to his Magyar overlords.

Soon after his ennoblement, he brought his father's body from the church at Scheii Brasqvolui to inter in the tower at Vlaicu, and about the same time obtained permission from John Hunyadi, then regent in Hungary, to extend his fortifications. It is from this time that the power of the Vlăhuțas began.

Unlike his father, the new count was no warrior at heart; he sought instead to consolidate his power through diplomacy and by whatever other means presented themselves to him. Before long, his choice of means took a curious and unwholesome turn. At the age of twenty-five, he married a Hungarian noblewoman, Márta Rákóczy, and through her

gained access to the court. Her family, as is well-known, later grew to great power in Transylvania, where they ruled as *voivodes* and princes. The line is still highly esteemed.

Some say it was from Márta that Count Matei learned the black arts, others that he had them from the Turks, or that a Jewish rabbi of Braşov sold him a certain book for five thousand talers. Whatever the source of his unholy knowledge, the count dedicated his life from that time onwards to two things: the preservation of his power and the prolongation of his life. When Márta died, he was already fifty-five, but it is said that she continued to instruct him for the next seventeen years.

Count Mani died at the age of seventy-two, and was laid to rest alongside his wife and father in the great vault beneath the tower at Castel Vlaicu, that had been built by Iordache at its inception. He was dead but, like his wife Márta, not truly dead. His body remains in its coffin at Castel Vlaicu, but it does not rot there. I have heard that there are no bones in the tombs of the Vlăhuţas save those of Iordache alone, who died as all men die, and is with his Saviour, alone of his tribe.

They say that, on the night of Matei's death, his eldest son, Antim, was seen in the cemetery at Satu Vlaicu. Since then, the people of that village have lit lamps by night on the graves of the recently deceased.

28

Translation of part of a letter in Ottoman Turkish to His Excellency, Count Vasile Vlăhuţa at Castel Vlaicu

20 BIRINCI TERŞIN 1649

I beg to inform your most excellent presence of the imminent despatch of a further shipment of Hungarian children surplus to the requirements of the devşirme levy recently conducted in the beylerbeyilik of Budin. You may be sure that these are all Christian children of the best quality, among whom are several originally destined for service in the Palace of the Sublime Porte as isoğlans of the top rank, and others intended for the Janissary corps on account of their physical perfection.

Our mutual friend, the timar defterdâri, has indicated to me personally that no account of these boys has been made by the Janissary officer responsible for the levy, and that he has been paid well by our friend himself. His payment I will see to today. As for myself, you know my situation and my gratitude for your former kindnesses.

The rumours that caused so much trouble formally have been quashed. There will be a payment, but not much. If your honour prefers, I will take care of the matter in my own way. It is all one to me.

I await your instructions, and assure you, as always of my desire to serve your excellency and your most noble and honoured family.

29

EXTRACT FROM THE JOURNAL OF
MIHAI VLĂHUȚA

14 December, late afternoon

Decay everywhere. Plaster crumbles from the walls. It is too cold for spielers, but I see webs beneath every ceiling, in fissures and cracks, across windows, as though the castle were slowly being wrapped in silk and dust as an offering.

We have not found Nicu. Liliana and I searched again today, but he does not show himself.

Liliana says she has found a manuscript history of the Vlăhuțas, and that I should read it. The author was a monk from Prislop monastery in Hațeg, Anghel de la Afumați, who visited Castel Vlaicu in 1757 at the invitation of my ancestor, Count Alexandru. He was responsible for the translation of the Turkish letter she showed me yesterday.

I do not wholly understand why she has become so interested in my family and its history. We seem to hold some fascination for her, and I begin to wonder if it may not be part of her plan. The Romanian tourist trade has made the most of Vlad Ţepeş, the supposed original for Dracula, and I imagine Liliana thinks it wouldn't do any harm to create some sort of sinister legend round Castel Vlaicu. I'd probably go along with her scheme if it weren't for feeling so betrayed. And if I didn't think it might be a little too close to the truth.

Notes from Liliana Popescu's 'Michael Feraru/Mihai Vlăhuța' File (undated)

The man Mihai saw was not Nicu. Today, Elena asked me why we were calling Nicu's name all through the castle. I told her, and when I finished Elena shook her head slowly.

'His name is Sergiu. He was my lover once.'

'Your lover?' I knew she had had a son, but the thought of a lover surprised me.

'Yes. Do you think I was not beautiful once? That I could not see? Sergiu loved me when I was eighteen. That was fifty-six years ago.'

I said nothing. I thought she must be raving. The figure Mihai said he had seen was that of a young man, no more than twenty-five.

She looked at me. With those unseeing eyes of hers, she looked at me, and I felt a chill pass through me, guessing, almost knowing what she was about to say.

'You think I have lost all sense of time?' she said. 'That I do not know what I am saying? Sergiu died when he was twenty-four, here in Castel Vlaicu. But he has never left me. I see him every day and every night. In a long black coat and military boots. He has long hair and a small black beard. That is the man Count Mihai saw.'

I asked her how she could see him, since she is blind, but I did not fully understand her answer. Sergiu is not a spirit, nor is he physically present, and she sees him with some sort of inner vision. And yet, she says, he is visible to the naked eye when the viewer is inwardly prepared. I asked her if she thought I might be able to see him. She shook her head.

'Not yet,' she said. 'You are not ready. But I think you may be very soon. Already you can hear them whispering. Soon you will begin to see them.'

'Them?'

'The *strigoï*. They that are dead and yet remain alive.'

I shivered. In my childhood, I had heard the word, whispered between adults. The *strigoï*. The undead. Not vampires, something worse, much worse.

'And when I see them, what then?'

She hesitated for a long time, as though deep in thought, buried in whatever inward world it is she inhabits. When she returned that blank gaze to me, I wondered what she saw.

'Then,' she said, very slowly, in that louche accent of hers, 'you will wish wholeheartedly you had never set foot inside Castel Vlaicu or ever known Count Vlăhuţa.'

31

EXTRACT FROM THE JOURNAL OF
MIHAI VLĂHUŢA

15 December

_____

I have read Father Anghel's account from beginning to end. I wonder now who the old man in my dreams may be. Is he Count Matei, or another of my ancestors, neither alive nor dead, but something in between? I saw him again last night. He smiles and chatters form-lessly, as if hoping I will finally understand something now beyond my grasp. There was someone else with him, a man of similar age, and so like the first in appearance that he might have been his son.

At least I know now what lies behind that door at the foot of the tower.

32

EXTRACT FROM THE JOURNAL OF
MIHAI VLĂHUŢA

15 December

'What was the *devşirme*?'

Liliana and I were eating breakfast together this morning. I had
been re-reading the Turkish letter in the light of Father de la Afumaţi's
chronicle. She screwed up her eyes and pursed her lips and thought
for a while.

'I'm not altogether sure,' she said. 'I remember being taught something about it in school. It was some sort of Ottoman institution.'

'A levy of some kind.'

'That's right. Oh, I know, the Turks used to take Christian children
from different parts of the empire and send them to Constantinople,
where they'd be trained as pages or civil servants. But most of them
ended up as soldiers, in the Janissary regiment.'

'So it was really a form of slavery?'

'In a way, though the harder-used slaves were mainly prisoners of
war. This was a little different, more like conscription. Some of the

boys rose to high office. They became Muslims first, of course, they were made to convert as children. I do remember reading that some even went on to become important Muslim religious leaders. They never saw their homes or their families again, of course. From the day they were taken, they belonged to the sultan.'

'How could one of my ancestors have arranged to be sent shipments of them? Surely the empire was better run than that?'

'Yes, but it was also corrupt. We were taught a lot about that in school, it was presented as justification for Romanian nationalism. The high state offices were up for sale. It was a rotten system, especially later on.'

'How long did this *devşirme* last?'

She shrugged. Her dark eyes scrutinized my face, as though eager for clues. But she knew what I was thinking.

'No idea. I don't think it went on as long as the last century, maybe not even to the eighteenth. I really don't know.'

I hesitated to ask her more. What I really wanted to know was – what had my ancestors done when the supply of boys dried up, as it must have done at some point?

33

Extract from the Journal of Mihai Vlăhuța

16 December, 3.00 a.m.

Liliana is with me again. She came to my room shortly after midnight, pounding on the door, demanding to be let in. When I opened the door, she was shivering, less from cold than fear. She took a long time to tell me what had frightened her.

'There is whispering every night,' she said, 'terrible whispering. I can't stand it any longer. All those voices. Sometimes they speak at once, sometimes a single voice comes close, right up to my ear. Men's voices mostly, but sometimes women, even a few children. The children are the worst, Mihai. They say such paltry, childish things, but they talk about horrors. They're older than you or me, far older, but they're still children. The dead do not grow old. The children of the *strigoï* do not advance in years.'

I tried to stop her, thinking it all madness. Yet I had read Father de la Afumaţi's record, and I wonder if madness and sanity mean anything in this dreadful place.

She got into bed with me, cold, shivering, and lost. I could not turn her away, or mock her, or refuse her. To be truthful, I wanted her. All that day, her body had tormented me like a whip. We made love slowly, as if we loved each other. Later, she told me what Elena had said about the figure in the corridor, that he was the ghost of an old lover of hers called Sergiu. I do not know whether to believe her or not. I almost feel I tricked her into her confessions about Nicu, with my story about the man I saw. But by the time spring is here, she will have forgotten all about him, and we will be happy again.

34

EXTRACT FROM THE JOURNAL OF MIHAI VLĂHUŢA

17 December

We woke early, and spent the morning in the library. Liliana went over Father de la Afumaţi's memoir with me, explaining sections I had not been able to understand before. It takes the family history up to the date of writing, in the lifetime of Count Alexandru, who died five years later, at the age of sixty-nine. From Father Anghel's introduction, it is clear that he was invited to Castel Vlaicu by Alexandru himself, and commissioned to write a history of the Vlăhuţa line.

The choice of de la Afumaţi for this task seems to have been prompted by the man's reputation as a biographer and historian. Liliana has found a nineteenth-century study of Romanian historiography, in which over a page is devoted to the priest and his published works. Historical writing in Romanian had expanded rapidly during the seventeenth century, reaching a sort of climax with the histories of Dimitrie Cantemir, a prince of Moldavia who was de la Afumaţi's teacher. The priest's first work, *Letopiseţul ţarii Moldovei*, a chronicle of Moldavian history, is dedicated to the prince.

De la Afurmaţi disappeared without trace in 1757, the year of his visit to Castel Vlaicu, and Liliana thinks it probable he never returned from here. It is highly likely he was asked to write his family history by Alexandru as part of the count's endeavour to placate his enemies at court.

Austria had annexed Transylvania in 1711, and by the middle of the century Hungarian influence was on the wane. Father Anghel's history states very clearly that the Vlăhuţas had acquired a black reputation by this time. Their links to the Hungarian nobility no longer had the power to protect them from the consequences of the ill name they held.

Alexandru must have been frightened that the Habsburgs would take away his castle and lands, for they had as little sympathy for Romanians as the Magyars before them. De la Afumaţi's preface dedicates the chronicle to the Archduchess Maria Theresa and her Chancellor, the redoubtable Kaunitz, and it seems entirely plausible that its purpose was to present the ruling powers with a highly cosmeticized version of life at Castel Vlaicu. Alexandru seems to have been greatly mistaken in his priest. De la Afumaţi must not have been corruptible, for his account of the Vlăhuţas makes very uncomfortable reading indeed. No wonder his manuscript was consigned to the library here, and that its author does not seem to have left Castel Vlaicu alive.

We have decided that the only way we can test de la Afumaţis wilder assertions is to investigate the family crypt, if we can manage to find the key. Elena is still adamant that she has none in her possession. If necessary, I shall order the door broken down by Costin, but that should only be done as a last resort.

35

EXTRACT FROM THE JOURNAL OF
MIHAI VLĂHUŢA

18 December

Ever since Liliana and I arrived here, Costin has demonstrated a murky resentment of us – especially me. He seems to suspect our intentions, and appears convinced we mean him and his mother some grave harm; our best efforts to win him over have gone unheeded or have been rebuffed.

The longer I spend with him, the more convinced I am that, far from being retarded, Costin is actually extremely bright. Of course, my original assumption had a lot to do with the impression his good looks made on me. His behaviour doesn't do much to win him friends or convey intelligence. He's taciturn, slow of speech, given to sulks. His moods are rapid in onset but long in duration, and I've seen him come close to a smouldering rage that might, once ignited, prove dangerous in such narrow confines as these.

But behaviour isn't everything. Costin is not in the least bit dull, but he is severely under-stimulated, and I think his pent-up anger stems almost wholly from a deep and unalleviated sense of frustration. There are moments when I see that this is a man of normal or perhaps even above-average intelligence, who has spent his entire life (as far as I can tell) in conditions confined enough to wreak havoc with even the strongest character.

Trapped behind these cold stone walls, which are almost all he has ever known of the world, Costin has dedicated his life to serving his mother and acting as her eyes. He has never been taught to read or write, he goes down to the village once or twice a year for provisions – a transaction which, I have been told, is carried out with the minimum of conversation, and wholly without charity or affection – he has no friends, no pets, no companionship beyond that afforded by his mother. And yet he remains pitifully devoted to her, and I have no doubt he would protect her at the cost of his own life.

He follows me everywhere he can, unless explicitly commanded not to. Even then he will eventually appear, under this or that pretext, in the hope of seeing what I am up to. He asks no questions, makes no comments; but his curiosity is blatant, and I have found that, as time passes, he is more and more willing to stand and listen while I tell him my plans or describe my thoughts.

He drinks it all in avidly, above all what I find to tell him of my travels, and of my life in England. My stories of my mother awaken the keenest interest in him, and he will sit for hours now, mesmerized by the most insipid anecdotes. His surliness and suspicion are slowly being pushed out by an almost childlike eagerness to learn of the world from which he has been cut off for so many years. I pity him more with every day that passes. And one day, I am certain, he will begin to tell me about himself and the life he has led here.

36

Letter from Count Tudor Feraru-Mavrocordato, Casă Feraru, Iași, to Count Miron Vlăhuța, Castel Vlaicu

19 Februarie 1786

Stimate și dragă var meu,
My esteemed and dear cousin,

The Greek is unwilling to accept your price, and says he must have more. I endeavoured to bargain with him, but to no avail. He will have his talers or you must go elsewhere. He knows too much, so I do not press him too hard.

Since the Russians annexed the Crimea, the Tatar khans send no more slaves to Constantinople. A few come in from the Caucasus, but as Russian influence spreads in the region, so the numbers dwindle. I have told him you will not have blacks, though he grumbles and says they are men like ourselves: a radical, this Greek of ours, but a greedy one.

Fortunately, our Phanariot relations at Sofia continue to turn a blind eye, and our friend believes he can send one or two hundred Bulgarian children a year. There is still a demand for slaves in Anatolia, and the trade will not slacken for some time yet. I have stressed to the Greek that you must have them alive, and I think he understands, or thinks he does.

My father, Stefan, has been ill these seven days and more. He says it may soon be time for him to make his final journey to rejoin his arcestors. Remember your promise, and give the word. Speak to Matei if you can, and obtain his consent. The doctors do not give him long, and there is the journey to be considered.

I await your instructions.

cu toată stima,

Tudor

37

EXTRACT FROM THE JOURNAL OF
MIHAI VLĂHUŢA

19 December

I saw Elena's lover again this evening. Liliana was with me, and though she did not see him, she says she heard him quite distinctly, walking across the floor of the library towards us. He looked distressed, as though tormented by thoughts or feelings he had carried with him beyond life and could not now expunge.

I tried to speak to him, using his name, Sergiu, but he ignored me, walking directly towards Liliana. He came to the table behind which she was sitting, and stood staring at something. I thought at first it was one of the books with which Liliana had been working, but when I looked more closely, I saw that his attention was fixed on the doll. He reached out a hand, as though to pick it up, then drew it back again as the impossibility of his gesture made itself evident. As he did so, he stared at Liliana, then at me with a look of the most terrible pain and loss, mixed with entreaty. He moved his mouth, as though speaking, but I could hear nothing.

Returning his gaze to Liliana, he mouthed a phrase over and over again to her.

Neither of us moved. The air in the library had grown ice cold, although the fire was still burning fiercely in the grate. I have never seen a man look more anguished. Liliana's face was racked with silent sobs, as though she wanted to help him, but could not. He stopped speaking, and looked down once more at the doll.

At that moment, we heard something. A child's cry, the selfsame cry I had heard in Bucharest, in that room in Casă Feraru, a piercing cry that shrank in moments to a low whimper. I looked round, almost expecting to see a child in the library, but there was nothing but heavy shadows. When I looked back, Sergiu had gone, and Liliana was cradling the doll in shaking arms.

Later, when she had calmed down and I was feeling steadier, we talked about what we had seen and heard.

'What did he say to you?' I asked. 'I couldn't make it out.'

She looked at me almost with the same despair that I had seen in Sergiu's face.

'*Trebuie să plecaţi Castel Vlaicu,*' she answered. 'You must leave Castel Vlaicu.'

38

EDITED TRANSCRIPT OF TAPE-RECORDED NOTES MADE BY MIHAI VLĂHUŢA

'It's . . . four in the morning on the twentieth of December. I don't feel . . . Just a moment.

[PAUSE.]

'No, it's all right, it's gone, only . . .

[PAUSE.]

'Something's been in our bedroom. We stayed up till very late, talking about what had happened, trying to make sense of Sergiu's warning to leave Castel Vlaicu. It was . . . I suppose it must have been well after midnight when I fell asleep.

'I don't know what woke me. All I remember is becoming totally alert in a matter of moments, and the second I did so I knew we weren't alone. Liliana was already awake. She must have . . . I suppose she could sense I was awake as well, because the next thing I heard her speaking to me quietly.

'"What is it, Mihai? Can you see? For God's sake, Mihai, what is it?"

'I was frozen with fear. God help me, but . . . I'm still frightened. I hadn't seen anything, hadn't . . . heard anything, but I could sense something in the room. It was overwhelming. We could both feel it. From the first instant, I knew it wasn't Sergiu. Neither of us had been frightened by him, but this thing, whatever it was . . . it just scared us shitless.

'I remember pulling myself up in bed. It was pitch dark, and I was straining hard to see, but I just couldn't make out a thing. Not a sodding thing. The presence made no sound. Not that it needed to. I honestly think . . . well, if I'd gone on just lying there like that much longer, I think I could have had a heart attack or something. I knew I had to do something, so I reached . . . I just stuck my hand out in the dark and grabbed the matches and struck one. My hand was shaking like a bastard, but I managed to get the lamp lit. It doesn't sound like much, putting your hand out in the dark like that, but I can tell you, it was the hardest thing I've ever had to do.

'It doesn't give much light, that lamp, but it was enough, really. I could make out most of the furniture and stuff, and nothing seemed out of place. The light stayed steady. The flame just sort of stayed there, as if it was holding its breath. You'd expect some shadows moving, but no, nothing. I . . . I remember I was holding my breath tightly, and looking all round the room as though I'd see something terrible the next moment. But . . . there was nothing. That's what's so fucking awful about this.

'"There's nothing," I said.

'"It's still here," whispered Liliana.

'It was cold. Really cold. The fire was dead, and there was heavy frost outside. We just lay there, and we knew there was something in the room with us, and we knew it was watching us, but we couldn't see a thing, not a damned thing. I even tried speaking to it, I think I was half mad, I said, "Who's there?", you know, the way you might do in a place you thought someone was waiting for you, but you couldn't see them or anything. I just kept saying it, over and over, "Who's there? Who's there?", but nobody answered, even though we both knew there was something, there had to be something, all this fear couldn't come from nothing. The only thing moving in the room, the . . . only thing that seemed alive . . . was our breath, great white clouds of it floating in front of our faces, changing shape, twisting as though it might take on some sort of concrete form any moment . . . For a long time I . . . couldn't take my eyes off it, I just kept on watching it, thinking it was about to solidify, but it never did, it just hung there, went on shifting till my eyes grew tired and I wanted to look away, and I did that, I looked away, and the next thing, all at once, Liliana said, "It's gone," and I looked at her, and I knew she was right, it had gone.

'We haven't slept since. I'm recording this, for I think something may happen, and I want to find some way to warn anyone who may come here looking for us in the spring. It's still freezing cold. We haven't any logs for the fire, and dawn's still a few hours away.

'It's four thirty. Still no sleep . . . Nothing has reappeared, but there's a sound of banging, as though someone in another part of the castle's thumping on a door. It goes on and on for minutes at a time, then stops, then starts again. Each time it starts, Liliana and I sit here terrified, praying it'll go away. I don't . . . Oh, God, it's started again . . .
    [MUFFLED BANGING.]
'A quarter past five. More banging, but weaker this time. It seems to reverberate through everything. I wish I were anywhere but here.'

39

EXTRACT FROM THE JOURNAL OF
MIHAI VLĂHUŢA

20 December, afternoon

We told Elena of last night's encounter with Sergiu. She listened intently, nodding at everything both of us said.

What did he mean when he said we should leave Castel Vlaicu?' I asked her. It is uncomfortable speaking with her. Her eyes stray here and there, but every so often she seems to stare directly at me, as though she can see after all.

'He meant that we are all in danger while we remain here. You most of all,' she said, meaning Liliana. 'But not you,' she continued, putting her hand on mine, almost with affection, I thought. 'Whatever happens, they will not harm you. You are the count, you are their guarantee that the Vlăhuţa line will continue. They will keep you safe at all costs.'

'I don't understand,' I protested. 'Who are "they"? Why should they protect me and harm you or Liliana?'

'She means the *strigoï*,' Liliana said. Her voice was flat. Since last night she has behaved like an automaton. All the emotion has been drained from her, all the fire.

'Vampires?'

She shook her head.

'No, not vampires. This is a serious business, Mihai – try not to make fun. The vampires you speak of are merely an invention, something from your Hollywood, dreamed up to frighten children and girls without sense. What we speak of is not material, at least not in the way your childish vampires are tied to their bodies and live or die with them. The *strigoï* exist in the spirit, but they are not ghosts. Their bodies remain in the tomb, undecaying, undead, yet not living. One cannot exist without the other. They walk, but it is not their bodies that walk.'

She hesitated. I could see that it troubled her to speak of such things. After the visitation of the previous night, I could not blame her.

'I can't explain this well, Mihai. Please forgive me. Elena knows more than I do. Ask her to tell you what it is we're living with.'

It was a long time before words came to Elena's mouth. She seemed to have gone far in search of them. They were simple words, but they seemed to have spent long ages in a place I cannot even imagine, a place where death and life are reversed, and light and darkness, and heaven and hell.

'They are the dead of the Vlăhuţas,' she said. 'Some have been dead centuries, others I have seen and spoken with. They live in darkness, wrapped in their tombs, but they do not wither in them, just as Liliana has said. The oldest among them are the strongest, and the longer they endure the stronger and more fearful they grow.

'For many years now they have been weak, but now you have come, their strength is starting to return.'

Her blind eyes rolled left and right, seeing nothing, seeing everything.

'They will not let you leave here,' she said. 'However long you live, they will not let you go as your father and his father went, abandoning them to their tombs.'

'I can still leave,' I said, though in my heart I had already started to believe her. 'It's a short descent back down to the village. From there, a day's journey will take us to Silistraru.'

Elena did not answer immediately. She stood at last and came right up to me. Stretching out one hand, she found my head and drew it towards her, kissing me on the forehead.

'Go to the window,' she said.

I did as she asked. When I looked out, there was only white. The heaviest snow of the winter had started to fall. As I write, I can hear a blizzard gain in strength outside.

'It is too late,' Elena said. 'You will never leave Castel Vlaicu.'

40

EXTRACT FROM THE JOURNAL OF
MIHAI VLĂHUȚA

20 December, evening

Elena left us to ourselves after that. She went to join Costin in their store, to sort through the food we will need for the coming week, and we retired to my sitting room, in order to talk over our predicament. In spite of the weather, I was still set on my plan. At the very least, I am sure we can make it to the village and wait there for a calm spell, when we will surely be able to persuade someone to take us as far as Silistraru, or maybe another village in the opposite direction. The main thing is to get as far away from here as possible.

In the event, we talked very little. Instead, we sat huddled round a listless fire, poking it from time to time, and exchanging unhappy glances.

It was much later when we heard a knock on the door, and Costin came in. He had been with us earlier, when we talked over the situation with Elena, but had remained silent throughout. It has crossed my mind more than once to wonder how he and his mother have managed to survive here all these years, surrounded day and night by God knows what horrors. She is blind, and, though she may see her beloved Sergiu from time to time, is, no doubt, protected from the worst. He, on the other hand, has spent his entire life here; I wonder he is not entirely deranged by it.

He was carrying something in his hands, carefully, like a child with a precious toy. Crossing to us, he set down on the floor a wooden box. It contained his treasures, he said. Would we like to see them? We nodded encouragingly, and he lifted the lid.

Inside, the cluttered remnants of somebody else's life: ribbons, medals, a wax flower, a locket containing strands of dark hair, letters carefully folded into faded blue envelopes, a pair of white kid gloves made for a small woman's hand, buttons – some silver, some enamel, some ivory, a tortoiseshell card case, a French painted fan.

He unwrapped a sheet of tissue paper to reveal a circular perfume bottle. It was empty, but still wore a gold label tied round the neck, bearing the name of the perfume, 'Le Baiser du Faune', and beneath that the legend 'Molinard: Paris/Grasse'. A medallion in the centre showed a faun kissing a forest nymph, and was signed 'R. Lalique'. I removed the stopper and placed the bottle to my nose. A faint perfume rose, as though summoned up from fifty or more years ago.

One at a time, Costin went through his treasures with us, telling stories connected to each of them. He had them pat, anecdote after pitiful anecdote, not one of them his own, all his mother's cast-offs, the detritus of a life already as good as over by the time he was born.

He knew the names of people long dead as well as a child might have had those of newly made friends, he could describe a woman's dress or a man's waistcoat as freshly as though he had just been with its wearer in the next room. The details of forgotten balls and long-silent parties tripped from his tongue as easily as they might fall from the lips of a dedicated playgoer newly come from the theatre.

In lieu of the life he had never led, Costin had been given his mother's to watch, as in a glass. As he picked up each of his treasures and related the incidents associated with it, we saw a different Elena than the one we had imagined. Liliana, at least, had guessed a little of the truth, as she told me later. But to me, who had seen none of the clues, it came as the most astonishing revelation. Elena was no country girl, brought up in the Carpathians by peasants and set to slave from an early age in a nobleman's castle. Her memories were all of Bucharest and the glittering social life she had known there as a girl and young woman, before the Communists had snatched her world away.

At the bottom of his box, Costin kept a small packet of his most precious possessions: some twenty or thirty photographs, fading now, and cracked, the survivors of a family album long ago lost or destroyed. They were individual portraits mainly, or groups, some formally posed, others more relaxed. In her blindness, Elena had guided her little boy through them, naming the sitters, identifying the rooms or houses in the backgrounds, remembering the occasions when each photograph had been taken.

Costin, I know, was innocent of all subterfuge. He had brought his treasures to us as a child might, in the hope of pleasing us, no more than that. He rehearsed his names and dates in the same way he had recited his litany of long-vanished Bucharest. He did not notice my reactions, could not, I am certain, have understood the significance of what he showed me. Not even Liliana grasped it at first, not until I spelled it out to her.

The photographs Costin laid out on the table before me were not just the scraps from someone else's past they had at first seemed. With a sensation of mounting bewilderment, I saw paraded before me

207

faces I knew from my own collection of family portraits. I recognized my grandfather, my grandmother, assorted aunts, uncles, and cousins. My father too was there, once as a little boy (in a duplicate of a picture my mother had sent), mostly as a young man.

In several of these photographs, there was a little girl, dark-haired, pretty, and mischievous-looking. She reappeared in later pictures as an adolescent and, briefly, as a young woman of eighteen or thereabouts. I had seen her before, in other family photographs, always with the caption 'Cousin Eniko'. But Costin gave her another name. He called her Elena, and identified her as his mother. And more than that, much more. He pointed to my grandparents, all the while not knowing that they were anything to me, and called them his own grandparents. And he pointed to my father and said, 'This is my mother's older brother, Dumitru.'

41

Extract from the Journal of Mihai Vlăhuța

20 December, midnight

I have just come from Elena. She has told me as much as I could bear to hear in one night. If there is a God, how He must hate my family. Or should we, perhaps, hate Him, because He has allowed us to exist?

'I was your father's sister and his closest friend,' Elena said. I suppose I ought to call her Aunt Elena. 'I was six years older, so I was a little mother to him when he was small. Dumitru was to be the next count, and I . . .'

She hesitated, smiling, a faint smile that took her back to a past I could not begin to imagine. The smile altered her face, as though years had been sloughed off, like old skin.

'I was to be even greater than a count,' she went on. 'A princess, my father always said, perhaps even a queen. I was a favourite of Queen Marie, and your grandfather saw to it that I spent as much time as possible at Cotroceni Palace. Her eldest son, Carol, was king by then, of course, so she was only a dowager; but the people loved her, and father knew she could be the key to his ambitions. She had some influence over her grandson Mihai, who was almost the same age as myself. When we were teenagers, Mihai and I spent a lot of time together. There were rumours of a romance.

'Well, it all came to nothing. Marie died in 1938. Not long after the war started, Carol was forced to abdicate, and Mihai became king. He had more important things to do than preoccupy himself with a silly girl. And, while it might have been just possible for a prince to marry a commoner, for a king it was out of the question.

'After that, father lowered his sights, but he still hoped to marry me off to someone important, someone with the influence to protect the family if the balance of power shifted. I was taken to balls and receptions, concerts and soirees. Because I was pretty, I attracted a lot of attention from young men; but father always managed to warn them off. The Vlăhuțas have a bad reputation, it was not so very difficult.

'In the end, he settled on one man, Corneliu Bibescu. Bibescu was the head of the National Christian Alliance, a political party which had the ear of the king. This was before 1944, when King Mihai overthrew Antonescu and joined the war on the side of the Allies. My father thought something of the sort would happen, and he was convinced Bibescu would be the next prime minister. Better than that, he might well decide to chuck Mihai out and proclaim himself dictator. I can't comment on the politics of the thing, or whether Bibescu was a good man or bad. All I cared about at the time was that he was almost seventy years old.'

She paused, as though the mere mention of Bibescu's age had served to bring into focus the reality of her own years. She is over seventy now herself, older than the would-be suitor of her youth. Her sightless eyes turned in my direction, not quite on me, not quite missing me. They were expressionless, but her face was soft and mournful.

'Your father hated him, of course. He came to my room one night in tears, crying that it was cruel to marry me off to "that old thug". That was his name for Bibescu.' She smiled. 'He hated him, you know, from the first moment he set eyes on him, or perhaps from the moment he was told I was to be his bride. He was only twelve then, but not at all a child. Our father made sure of that, made sure Dumitru behaved like a man from the earliest age. He was fearfully stern, particularly with my brother. Did your father ever tell you that?'

I shook my head. Nothing had ever been said, nothing so much as hinted at. I thought back to the years when I had known my grandfather, until his death when I was fifteen. He was often aloof, sometimes locked inside his own world, but never, to my knowledge, harsh or unkind or stern. I remembered only his kindnesses to me, and put the rest down to what pride there remained to him of ancestry and rank. A kindly, proud old man, I used to think. And here was my aunt, describing a petty tyrant.

'Father met Bibescu several times to talk about terms for an engagement,' she went on. 'It was a simple trade-off. Bibescu needed an aristocratic wife to cement his political career, my father wanted to hitch the Vlăhuţa horses to the juggernaut of far-right politics. I was just the coin my father paid. But it didn't matter, not really.

'Before a betrothal could be finalized, I had fallen in love. You know his first name already, Sergiu. Sergiu Averescu. He was an army officer, a captain who'd been wounded at the Front and sent back to Bucharest to recover. He wasn't seriously hurt, so he was given a desk job in the capital. We met at a concert at Ana Brucan's house. She introduced us. I think she knew about Bibescu and wanted to see me safe with a younger man. Well, whatever she planned, it worked.'

Elena paused again, and I thought she smiled at someone. I looked round, but there was no one there. Liliana listened in silence. Costin sat a little away from us. Did he know all this already, or was it all fresh to him?

'We fell in love with one another, as desperately and as hopelessly as any couple in such times. At any moment, Sergiu expected to be sent back to the Front. Or the Russians might invade, or the king might tell the Germans to leave and be attacked by them. Every day, we woke not knowing what that day would bring.

'When life is so uncertain, people do foolish things. Sergiu and I found plenty of opportunities to meet alone. Our affair was kept a dark secret from everyone, especially my father. Only Ana knew, and perhaps her husband. Of course, we could never meet as often as we wished, or stay together for as long as we would have liked. But it was the happiest time of my life. Until I became pregnant.'

She halted once more, as though out of breath. Sighing, she passed a hand across her eyes, as the sighted will do, as though to blot out something that troubled her.

'I kept it secret as long as I could, but in the end it all came out. My father demanded Sergiu's name, and when he discovered he was no one of any social worth, just a captain in the infantry, he had him posted to Transnistria, and from there to the Kuban Front.

'I stayed at home in Bucharest and had my baby. It was a boy, the most beautiful baby boy you can imagine. I called him Emil.'

For the first time since I had known her, Elena's face was transformed with something akin to radiance. Not only years fell away this time, but griefs and sadnesses and miseries beyond reckoning.

'Your father – my little Dumitru – used to come and play with him, you know. He adored him, and came to see him whenever he could, though he wasn't even supposed to know he existed.'

She looked pleadingly at me.

'Did he . . . did he ever say anything to you . . . about a baby? A nephew? Did he ever say he had a nephew called Emil?'

I shook my head again. My father had said nothing to me about an aunt or a cousin. I had grown up thinking my family in Romania all dead or vanished. Elena nodded, accepting my denial with long-practised resignation.

'I spent every day and every night with him,' she continued, 'and I dreamed of Sergiu and prayed he would be safe. Every day I waited for news of him. Ana came to visit me – father never knew of her involvement in the affair – and brought what news she could, which was little enough. There were regular casualty lists, and Ana would bring them for me to read. We both dreaded seeing Sergiu's name, but every time we got to the end and it wasn't there, it was like the most wonderful reprieve.

'Then a miracle happened, and I got a letter from him, through Ana. He said things were hard, but he would soon be due some leave and would plead with my father to be allowed to see me and his son. My mother had fallen in love with little Emil, and I asked her to speak to father on my behalf.

'That was when the second miracle happened, or so I thought. My father agreed to see Sergiu and to talk about the possibility of a marriage. Bibescu was finished by then, anyway: his party was in disarray, and whoever was going to be the next prime minister or president, it wasn't going to be him. Of course, father had also discovered that Sergiu's father, even if he wasn't an aristocrat, was enormously wealthy; it looked as though hard cash was going to be of much more benefit after the war than breeding.

'Sergiu arrived home a month later. He was thin and tired, and living on his nerves, but underneath he hadn't changed a bit. We were deliriously happy. Ana brought him round within an hour of his arrival, and we had the most wonderful reunion. Then he met mother, and finally father. He came the next night for dinner, and afterwards he and father went to the study and talked for ages. Sergiu came back to say we had been given permission to marry.'

She seemed half in a reverie. It had surely been the happiest moment of her life. But in her memory there also lay the horrors that had been born of it.

'Things weren't very pleasant in Bucharest in those days. We thought Sergiu might be sent back to the Front any day. Father spoke to a friend of his, a general, and a couple of hours later Sergiu had a post with the military legal affairs department in the city. It wasn't that he was a coward – he was willing to go back to the Front. But at that time we were fighting the Russians on behalf of the Germans, and Sergiu had no wish to lay down his life for Hitler.

'It was already late autumn, but father suggested that we should spend the remainder of Sergiu's leave at Castel Vlaicu. Away from Bucharest, he could recover from the strain of being at the Front. He was given permission to extend his leave by a month, and we got everything ready to go to the castle.

'It was to be my first visit. Does that surprise you? I had always wanted to go, but normally only my father and Dumitru were allowed. The mountains were too wild for women, I was told. But it wasn't that, of course. It was the castle itself.

'The day we left, my only unhappiness was that we had to leave little Emil behind. My father said the journey would be too rough for a baby. We would be forced to travel some of the way on horseback, and once we were in the mountain it would be cold. Emil was a delicate child. I left him with Doina, his nurse. It was the last I saw of him.'

She fell silent again. In the background, Costin was sobbing softly.

Elena was dry-eyed, but he wept, as though content to be, not only his mother's eyes, but her tears as well.

'Once we arrived here, my father changed. He scarcely spoke to me or to Sergiu. For hours at a time, he would keep to his room, reading and writing. Sometimes I would hear him speaking. I thought at first he spoke to himself, but in the end I came to understand the truth: that he was never alone, that none of us in Castel Vlaicu were ever alone.'

She sighed, and it seemed she listened, not to anything in the room, but to sounds throughout the castle, sounds I could not quite hear, could not quite ignore. I remembered my grandfather, that wretched, sad old exile, how he would come with us on holiday, to Scarborough or Whitby, for a day or a week at a time, and while the rest of us went out for walks or excursions, he would make his excuses and remain behind in his room, to read, he said, and to think.

I thought then it was only natural for the old to want solitude, but now I am not so sure, now I begin to wonder what thoughts they were exactly that he could not share with his own family.

'After a few days of this treatment,' Elena went on, 'Sergiu said we should go back to Bucharest. I wanted to go with him. The castle was dark and gloomy, and I felt quite depressed. Your father was kept away from us, and I missed his laughter and the silly conversations we would sometimes have. Sergiu felt we'd been tricked in some way, brought out here under false pretences, then left to our own devices. I was worried about Emil, and wanted to get back to him.

'Sergiu went to father and said he couldn't stay cooped up here any longer, that we had to go back to the capital the very next day. Father just smiled and said that was impossible, there was no transport to be had, not at the castle, not in the village. We didn't know what to believe. My mother was no help, and your father could do nothing, he was powerless against your grandfather.

215

'That night, the whispering began. You and Liliana have heard it, I know, though you do not understand it fully. I was sleeping alone, of course, and it frightened me half to death. I'm used to it now. You can get used to almost anything.

'I didn't sleep a wink that night. In the morning, I came down for breakfast, tired and on edge. Part of me thought I was going insane, another part knew I was not. When I got to the dining room, neither my mother nor Dumitru were there. I was told that they had gone down to the village to take money and clothes to the tenants' wives. Later, I noticed that the two maids my mother had brought from town were missing as well. But it was already evening by then, and it was already too late for questions or answers.

'My father's mood appeared to have mellowed once more. Over breakfast, he was talkative. He asked Sergiu about the fighting he had seen, and appealed for his opinion as to the outcome of the war. It was what we thought of as men's talk then, so I listened and made no comments on matters of which I had no direct knowledge. I only remember thinking that, when Emil grew up, I would not want him to be a soldier.

'By and by, Sergiu softened. My father apologized for his earlier behaviour, saying that his first days away from the city always saw him in bad spirits, as though all the negative feelings he had been storing up while in town were let loose by the country air.

'Soon, the conversation turned to our forthcoming marriage, and from there to Emil.

'"You know that Emil will be next in line after Dumitru, if I should have no more male children?" my father asked Sergiu. "His education can be taken care of easily enough. But I am concerned that you, as his father, understand the duties and responsibilities such a high position will entail."

216

'"I think I understand them well enough," Sergiu answered. It was the wrong reply, although I think it would have made no difference by then how he answered. It was all a game, after all. My father was making sport of him.

'My father shook his head. He was a grave man, full of his own importance, and the importance of his family.

'"No," he said, "I think you do not. Your family has only newly come by its money, and as yet it has no power or influence to speak of. We Vlăhuţas have been wealthy and powerful for centuries. Each one of us is the product of blood and training past your comprehension."

'He stood up suddenly, looking down at Sergiu. For a moment, I thought I heard more whispering. A shadow moved beyond my father's head, startling me. He glared at me, then looked back at Sergiu.

'"Come," he said, "I will show you what it is to be a Vlăhuţa."

'I thought for moment that Sergiu would refuse, that my father's arrogance would prove too much for him. But he loved me, and he would have swallowed anything to soothe my father's feelings and so seal our marriage. To this day I wish he had had more pride, pride enough to defy my father and leave Castel Vlaicu.

'My father took us to the door you've seen, the door at the foot of the tower. It leads to the vault where our tombs are kept. He had the key, a huge key, on a chain round his neck. I remember how it jangled when he took it out, how it vibrated in that stillness.'

I saw her shiver. Costin's sobs had subsided, but he still listened intently, as though hearing her story for the first time. I thought again of my grandfather, of that gentle man holding my hand as we walked through the park or along the quiet streets of Harrogate, an old man full of memories, and I imagined him grown suddenly hard and

217

overbearing. Was Elena telling the truth? Or had the years and blindness created monsters in her brain?

'We all carried lamps,' she went on, 'but in that darkness they made little impression. I hung back, half curious, half afraid. They were my ancestors, after all, I felt drawn to them by blood. But the proximity of so much death and darkness alarmed me.

'My father turned the key in the lock and drew the door back on hinges that had not been oiled since his own father was laid to rest there. I could see nothing inside but more darkness.

'"These are the tombs of the Vlăhuţa," he said to Sergiu. As he spoke, he gestured, indicating that Sergiu go ahead of him. Sergiu glanced at me, a quick, loving glance that I will never forget. The next moment, he turned and stepped inside the vault, holding the lamp high above his head to give him light. My father waited until Sergiu had descended a short flight of steps, then pushed the door shut with a great bang. I tried to stop him, but he had already turned the key.'

She sighed deeply.

'The door has never been opened since,' she said. Behind her, Costin shook his great head and stifled a sob. Had Sergiu been his father? I wondered. Costin and Emil were not the same person. I thought I already knew what had happened to little Emil.

'You cannot imagine how I struggled. My father had to summon one of the servants to help him overpower me. All I can remember is being dragged away while Sergiu beat on the door behind me. I can still hear that pounding in my dreams at times.'

I told her what Liliana and I had heard early this morning. She nodded wearily.

'Yes,' she said. 'In my waking hours as well. But when I am awake, I can stop my ears for as long as it continues.'

218

She made a gesture as of blocking her ears, then let her hands drop limply to her side, where they rested as though all life had been drained from them.

'But not when I sleep,' she said. 'I cannot stop it then.'

After a moment, she continued.

'I was locked in my room for over a week. Tiberiu, the servant, brought me food and drink every day, but I ate nothing. I was wretched, nearly out of my mind with misery and fear. My father did not come near me once. For the first few days, I could hear Sergiu pounding on the door. I howled and screamed, and threw myself at the door of my own room. But it was useless. Tiberiu took my trays away and brought fresh ones, but he was under orders to ignore my pleas for help. No amount of tears could make an impression on him.

'On the fourth day, the banging stopped. Sergiu's lamp would have lasted a few hours at most. I thought of him down there in the dark, going out of his mind. Of course, had I known then what I know now . . .'

I saw her shudder, and I knew that, however long her residence here, it had not brought her immunity to the horrors that surrounded her. And something told me every word she uttered was spoken from the heart, and from vivid memory.

'By the time I was allowed to leave my room, Sergiu was dead and I was a little mad. My mother and Dumitru had returned safely to Bucharest by then, and I had no one to turn to, no one who would comfort me. I don't know what my father told them, or whether he was believed.

'I was not allowed to leave – that was made clear to me on the first day out of my room. My father had dismissed any servants he thought might show sympathy for me or help me escape. This left Tiberiu, who was a scoundrel and a brute, his wife, who was little better, and a boy called Gabi, who was stupid and cruel.

'Father spent most of his time in his study. He communicated with me through the servants, sending verbal and written messages. We ate separately. The days passed, and my madness started to turn into something else. Hatred, I think, and a longing for revenge.

'Before long, winter set in. Father decided to return to Bucharest, rather than remain cooped up here until spring. The day before he left, he visited me in my room.

'"You must think me very harsh and very cruel," he said. I was at work on a piece of embroidery. It was a picture of dog roses, I remember. I continued sewing, paying him no attention. But I could hear him perfectly well.

'"If you must know," he went on, "I regret what has happened very much. If I had had any choice in the matter, your marriage would have gone ahead as planned. But you have to understand: you are not only my daughter, you are a Vlăhuța. We are none of us at liberty to love or marry as we please. There is more at stake than you can imagine. I'm not speaking of money or land or power. There are other things, more important things, of which you know nothing."

'He had brought Tiberiu with him. The oaf stood watching us without a flicker of emotion. I went on sewing.

'"But your ignorance cannot be an excuse for the destruction of what we are and what we may become. After what has happened, you cannot return to Bucharest. You will live out the rest of your days here in Castel Vlaicu. To be frank, I wanted you dead. But you are a Vlăhuța, and you are my daughter."

'I thought that was all, that he would go away and leave me by myself. I wanted nothing better than to be left alone. But he continued to look at me, as though steeling himself for what was to come. Out of the corner of my eye, I saw him nod to Tiberiu. The next moment, my arms were grabbed from behind, and Tiberiu was holding them hard. No matter how I struggled, I could not break his grip.

'My father bent to pick up the embroidery that had fallen from my lap. He set it to one side, but when he turned back to face me, I saw he was holding the needle between his fingers. A long strand of embroidery thread hung from one end. He stepped towards me and took my chin in the other hand, forcing my face up. It was at that moment that I realized what he was going to do . . .'

She broke off, lifting her hands to her mutilated eyes in a gesture of childish terror. Costin broke out sobbing. And I sat and watched her, and while I watched, remembered my grandfather's hand as it stroked my hair while I sat in his lap and listened to tales of old Bucharest.

42

Translation of part of a letter to Count Iuliu Feraru, Casă Feraru, Bucureşti
(among the papers of Count Mihai Vlăhuţa)

seară, 15 noiembrie 1936

My dear Iuliu,

All you requested has been done. I visited Matei earlier this evening and poke with him for above an hour. He is hungry, but counsels patience nonetheless. He says the boy must be made to understand, that he must not be pampered or allowed to forget who he is and what he must do in time.

One of the villagers died this week and was buried with candles and prayer that none might touch him. I watched from close by, but nothing was to be done. In recompense, a traveller was sent to us, a young man, amiable and quiet-spoken, a Hungarian of no consequence . . .

43

FROM A SHORT MANUSCRIPT HISTORY OF THE
VLĂHUŢA FAMILY BY FATHER ANGHEL DE LA
AFUMAŢI, CONTAINED IN A BOUND COLLECTION
ENTITLED *Documente privitoare la Barbu
Vlăhuţa (1737)*, AND DISCOVERED BY LILIANA
POPESCU IN THE LIBRARY AT CASTEL VLAICL

WHAT EVILS CAME of Count Matei's death and the
wickedness of the new count, Antim, I cannot fully
relate. Each of the Vlăhuţas in turn lives and dies
and joins the ranks of the undead, preying upon
the spirits of the newly deceased. With successive
generations, they have travelled further and further
afield to find corpses freshly interred, from which to
take ghastly sustenance. For the people of their own
valley know what it is they seek, and keep watch
by night to deter them. Nevertheless, there are those
that die suddenly and are unprotected. Above all,
they delight in the spirits of the infant dead, and
some say the living of the family procure for their

undead relatives a very particular nourishment from that source, not blanching to secure the early deaths of some that might have lived otherwise.

The dead live on in some form in their coffins, but it is their spirits that take food by these means, and it is their spirits that walk the castle and venture abroad by night. I have heard them myself, whispering and talking among themselves, and I fear that, if by some ill chance I should die here, my spirit shall not find rest. Those they feed on truly die and rot in the grave; but their spirits are forever tormented by these creatures.

44

EXTRACT FROM THE JOURNAL OF
MIHAI VLĂHUȚA

21 December

Costin came to our room this morning, very upset. He had not seen his mother since last night, could not find her anywhere. Liliana and I joined him, and together we searched all the main rooms of the castle, calling her name. We are all worried. A blind woman cannot get far, or so we reason. But this is not an ordinary place, and more than her life may be at risk.

We accompanied Costin back to the bedroom he shares with his mother. It is a pitiful chamber, sparsely furnished and cold. With so many rooms and so much fine furniture to choose from, it is hard to understand why Elena chose to stay here. She is blind, but surely that would not rob her of all sense of comfort.

Costin sat on the edge of the bed and talked. His anxiety for his mother was evident. She is, after all, the only other human being he has ever really known. His father was not Sergiu, as I had suspected. It seems that my grandfather left Elena in the castle to rot, guaranteeing her permanent incarceration less by means of locks than through her blindness. Tiberiu and his companions treated her harshly, but their orders were to feed and nurse her, and they understood too well the price of disobedience.

With time, she learned to find her way about the rooms and corridors. The boy, Gabi, was more considerate than his parents. He became her guide, and introduced her to many of the tricks and mechanisms she needed to fend for herself.

In 1947, my family left Romania for good, and Elena's plight worsened for a time. In the absence of my grandfather and his occasional visits to the castle, Tiberiu became ruthless towards his prisoner, beating her and depriving her of all but the most basic necessities. Things might have gone very badly for her indeed had Tiberiu and his wife not been as fearful of the undead as they had been of the living.

With my grandfather and father both gone, the task of seeking out new burials and worse fell to Tiberiu for a time. In 1949, the authorities requisitioned the castle and placed a caretaker in charge, a young man from Satu Mare called Viorica.

Viorica was a dedicated Communist, but a fair man who saw in Elena, not a despised aristocrat, but a fellow human being who had suffered greatly – though she never told him just how much. Tiberiu and the others were dismissed, and villagers brought in from Satu Vlaicu to clean and maintain the place. None ever stayed long, and Viorica himself was sorely tempted to follow them. But a sense of duty, combined with fear of his masters and a growing affection for Elena kept him at his post.

Elena never discovered exactly what it was Viorica had been sent to Castel Vlaicu to do. The chances are he never knew himself The castle had been taken from its undeserving, absent owners and handed to the Romanian people; in time the state would find a use for it, but until then it had to be cared for.

In time, Viorica and Elena became lovers. It's hard to know how much they really loved one another, and how far they were driven together by fear and pity. It scarcely matters. For a little time, at least, they must have given one another comfort.

Costin was born about eighteen months after Viorica first arrived. When the boy was eight, his father was summoned back to Satu Mare. He never returned, and no one was ever sent in his place. I don't know why he did not take Costin with him, but by then no one else would stay with Elena, and she would not leave the castle because Sergiu was there. With his father gone, little Costin devoted himself to what was to be his life's work, the care of his mother. The years passed, and he went from boyhood to middle age, but not once did he think to abandon her or to go in search of the father he could barely remember.

He had a weak heart, he said. It had been diagnosed by a doctor who had seen him as an infant, before his father's departure. His mother sometimes said he should leave Castel Vlaicu to seek treatment, but he always refused; without him, Elena would certainly die. He stayed and comforted her, and from time to time he would venture out to find sustenance for the *strigoï*. They left him little choice: as long as he brought them what they sought, Sergiu would be spared their torments.

Costin has gone. But before he went, he took something from his pocket and handed it to me: a heavy iron key, slightly rusted, and about six inches long. I have it beside me now, on my desk. A candle with a pale flame burns beside it, casting long, darting shadows across its surface. Soon, I think to myself, soon.

45

Notes from Liliana Popescu's 'Michael Feraru/Mihai Vlăhuţa' file (undated)

Mihai behaves more and more strangely the longer we remain here. It is as if he is shedding bit by bit whatever English traits he had acquired from his mother and his upbringing, and is putting on the garb of the Romanian aristocrat he might have been. Every day his language becomes purer, the accent less pronounced. I see his resemblance to his ancestors in those arrogant portraits that seem to hang in every corner of this place. I see it in his eyes above all, that same arrogance, that same cruelty.

At other moments, he seems his old self again. I begin to think that two distinct personalities are struggling for ascendancy within the same body – Michael and Mihai. But Mihai has the upper hand, I think, and in the end he must prevail.

46

EXTRACT FROM THE JOURNAL OF MIHAI VLĂHUȚA

22 December, late afternoon

We found Elena earlier this afternoon. Since she was not to be found anywhere in the castle, I concluded that she must have tried to leave. We all went outside, into the most penetrating cold I have ever experienced. There was a low mist that cut the valley off from us, making it seem that we and the castle were hanging suspended above white clouds. No sounds reached us from any direction.

She was lying in the snow several yards in front of the main gate, through which she must have left. Her body was cold, her hair frosted, her eyes open and staring, sightless now beyond all hope.

All around her, deeply imprinted in the otherwise virgin snow, were scores of crisply incised footprints.

'Wolves,' I whispered, bending to examine a line of tracks. When I straightened, Costin was looking at me. He shook his head. His eyes were still dumb with grief.

'No,' he said. 'Not wolves.'

47

EDITED TRANSCRIPT OF TAPE-RECORDED NOTES MADE BY MIHAI VLĂHUŢA

'It's the twenty-second of December . . . I don't understand. Why did you hate her so much? You were always kind to me, you never shouted, never got angry. There were times when my father lost his temper, and I'd come round to your house, and you'd listen to me, you and granny both. But Elena . . .

[INDISTINCT WHISPERS.]

'I see. No, I understand, at least I think I do. And what about my father?

[MORE WHISPERS.]

'I see. Yes, that: makes sense. And now? What do I have to do now?'

48

EXTRACT FROM THE JOURNAL OF
MIHAI VLĂHUȚA

22 December, evening

Elena's body has been left on a table in the vast white room that used to be the castle kitchen. It's as cold a spot as we could find at short notice. She'll be all right there until we can move her to the vault. Costin and I will take her there together later tonight: Liliana is too frightened to be of any use. In the absence of a coffin, we shall have to put her in several shrouds and hope that the cold there will preserve her until spring comes.

Her body is curiously unharmed. The most likely cause of death is exposure. Nothing attacked her. We looked carefully for signs of a wound, but there were none. When we brought her back, I asked Costin about the spoor we had found.

'Surely wolves are the only creatures who could leave tracks like that,' I said. I had had enough of people telling me there were no wolves here. I had heard them, seen their tracks in the snow, glimpsed their eyes in the forest; why was everyone so determined to deny their existence?

'You don't understand,' he said. 'The *strigoï* cannot leave the castle in their own bodies. They cannot inhabit two human bodies at once, so they are forced to use the bodies of wolves when they want to go elsewhere. In time, they change, in time they become more human than wolf. Some of them are old, extremely old. If you saw them near at hand, then you would know that no one has lied to you. They are not wolves, not any longer.'

49

Edited transcript of tape-recorded notes made by Mihai Vlăhuţa

'It's now late evening of the twenty-second and Liliana's in the library, reading. I don't want to disturb her. She says she read something in de la Afumaţi's manuscript about how the *strigoï* may be destroyed. The priest mentioned a book he'd seen in the library, a French book with instructions on how to destroy them. Apparently, he wouldn't make any use of it himself, since it involved practising magic. Liliana's trying to track it down, but I fancy she's too late. The *strigoï* are starting to come awake after their long sleep. I can hear them clearly, and I understand them perfectly at last. Now I know what it is they want me to do.'

50

Extract from the Journal of Mihai Vlăhuţa

22 December, late evening

Elena's body seemed as light as a bird's to carry. Costin and I managed easily enough between us, he weeping all the time, I conscious of the ironies of the situation. We carried her on a makeshift stretcher of boards, with as much dignity as we could summon. Our only light came from the lamps we had attached to the handles of the stretcher. Otherwise, all around us was dark. I could feel the shadows stretching beyond the walls and out into the night. As I expected, Liliana did not come.

As we came to the door, we laid Elena on the ground. It seemed a good idea to take a close look at the vault before we tried to carry her down. I still had the key Costin had given me. He had kept it by him all these years and never used it once. I feared the lock would have rusted, and that the key might now be useless. But it turned well enough, and the door swung open with barely any effort, as though it had been waiting for me.

At first, I could make out nothing but a raw and stinking blackness beneath me, as though the door had opened on to a pit from which nothing could escape, not even darkness. Beside me, Costin recoiled. I raised a lamp and swung it before me into the dark void. It showed nothing but a flight of stone steps at my feet, dull and dry and pitted with age.

'I'm going down,' I said. Costin did not answer. I was not afraid. They were my ancestors, after all. 'Wait for me here,' I said. He stood by his mother's remains, watching me like a child who fears to be left alone.

I put a foot on the stairs and, as I did so, heard, quite distinctly, a sighing sound somewhere below me in the dark. I told myself I was not afraid, and I do not think I was, not really; but my heart could not be so easily cajoled: it was beating fast, and my palms were slick with cold sweat.

There were twelve steps in all. I teetered for a moment on the last, uncertain whether or not I had indeed reached the bottom. Disoriented, I lifted the lamp.

All round me in a small space were the tombs of my forebears. They were not lined up along the walls in decent rows, as if in some well-ordered church, but distributed unevenly throughout the vault. Most were of stone, but others were nothing more than large, elaborately carved wooden coffins. These were older than the tombs, but perfectly preserved. Beneath centuries of encrusted spider web, the fine detail of their carving caught the little light shed by my lamp and gave it shape.

The air was thick and stale, almost noxious to breathe, yet infinitely colder than the air outside. A dark, disquieting odour filled my nostrils, making me gag. I thought at first it must be a stench of decay, but immediately realized the impossibility of it. Whatever this was, it could not be the after-smell of rotting flesh.

Not far from the steps, my light picked out a glimmer of something white. I stepped closer. Sergiu – what little was left of him – lay curled up where he had died, his soldier's uniform wrapping white bones, as though this was a battlefield beneath the earth. Strands of black hair clung to the skull like seaweed to a dry rock. His fleshless hands were empty. Spiders had ornamented him with uncompassionate skill.

I approached the first tomb, a stone rectangle incised with finely chiselled Roman letters, telling in Latin the virtues of its inhabitant. Looking more carefully, I deciphered the name: Alexandru. De la Afumați's count, and, for all I knew, his murderer. To my surprise, the tomb had no lid. I was repelled, but after all I had heard and read, I could not prevent myself from standing on tiptoe and looking over the edge.

Alexandru was still there, undecayed, yet horribly changed. He did not have the pale, waxen appearance of a corpse, nor the shrunken skin of someone who has been in the grave for a little while. Instead, his face was bloated and dark with blood, so dark, indeed, it was almost black. His lips were drawn back slightly from yellow teeth. His body, too, had swollen, splitting his clothes here and there, as though he had been feasting on death. As I stared at him, his eyelids opened and he returned my gaze with sharp, cruel eyes. Other than that, he did not move. Hurriedly, I stepped aside.

The other tombs and coffins had their own inhabitants, all bloated and dark, all conscious. As I stood among them, I could hear them begin to whisper between themselves. They knew who I was and why I was there.

I went back up the steps, knowing Costin would be growing anxious. He was there, waiting beside his mother's body, his face a sullen mask of grief. My heart was beating like a hand on wood; I knew what I still had to do, and I still recoiled from it.

'I've found Sergiu,' I said. 'If you like, we can put them together. Do you think your mother would have wanted that?'

I could see that the idea had not crossed his mind. He thought for a while, then nodded.

'Yes,' he said. 'They've always been together.'

We took her body off the stretcher and manoeuvred it carefully down the steps. I went first, holding her feet, and Costin after, taking her by the shoulders. The corpse was neither wildly rigid nor wholly flexible.

I had already picked out a spot for her in one corner. We laid her down delicately. The whispering had fallen silent. Costin avoided looking at the tombs. He was like a huge child, unwitting, trusting, without guile. I felt betrayal seep through me like a poison. My heart beat even faster. I could not back away from it now, it had become a sacred trust, a duty.

'Sergiu's over here,' I said. 'He'll just fall apart if we try to move him like this. I'll go back up for the stretcher.'

Elena had left the castle of her own volition, enticed by something she alone could see or hear. Costin would not venture out so readily, or remain there, waiting in the darkness for them to take him. I had to deal with him myself, and I knew it would not be easy.

As I turned to go, he looked at me. I smiled unsteadily. Before he could protest, I was at the steps. I started to climb.

'Don't leave me alone down here,' Costin said. 'I'm frightened.' He had never seen death like this before, never smelt it.'

'I won't be a moment,' I said. He was already heading for the steps. I hurried up, and he followed me, quickening his pace, guessing at last what I was about to do.

'No!' he shouted, rushing at me, his great body ready to crash into me. As he came level with me, I drew back my foot and kicked out,

237

striking him hard on the shin. He cried out, bending in pain, and I turned and made for the door. I dashed through it and slammed it shut, turning the key with a hand that shook like my heart. Seconds later, the door shivered as Costin struck it, and his voice came to me, high and wailing and filled with dread. Trembling, I turned my back and walked away, and behind me I heard the sound of his great hands hammering.

Liliana and I are back in the library. She is reading, while I am writing up this journal. She has found her book of spells, though I don't think it makes much sense. Every so often, she looks up and sighs, like a student who has suddenly discovered she is reading a subject for which she is poorly equipped. If Costin is still hammering the door of the vault, we cannot hear it: I took care to shut all the doors between us and him. It will be time for bed soon. Perhaps we shall hear something in the night. But it will not matter.

51

Note left at the British Consulate, Bucharest, by Miss Sophie Wandless

22 December

Oh, God, Michael, I don't know what to write. You have to get in touch, if you ever get this note. The vice-consul said he'd give it to you straightaway if you called in, or read it to you over the phone if you rang. But he says there are no phones where you are, and no means of getting out till spring.

Your mother . . . I'm sorry, you'll have to get in touch, I don't want to put this in writing, you shouldn't come to it cold, you have to ring, what will you do, what will you do? Something dreadful has happened, something I can't write about.

I tried to find you everywhere, and everywhere they said you'd gone, you'd disappeared. And then I met a young man, a trainee hotelier called Nicu. A woman at the university put me on to him, he's a friend of your lawyer, Liliana. He says you both left for the Carpathians a few weeks ago, that you must be there now. My God, Michael, why did you go to that place? Didn't you get any of my letters?

I'm going back to England, Michael, I can't wait here till spring. Get in touch the minute you read this note. I love you, Michael. I pray nothing happens to you.

Sophie

52

EDITED TRANSCRIPT OF TAPE-RECORDED NOTES
MADE BY MIHAI VLĂHUŢA

'I've done what you wanted, haven't I? What more is there? . . . No, you can't expect me to do that, I . . . There's no point, I can't, don't you understand? Yes, I know that, but . . . Please don't look at me like that . . .

[LONG PAUSE.]

'All right, I'll do it, and the other thing too. But after that, I want to be left alone.'

53

CLIPPING FROM THE *YORKSHIRE EVENING POST*, 23 DECEMBER

THE HARROGATE GUEST HOUSE TRAGEDY

Unconfirmed reports indicate that the death toil in the Queen Marie Guest House tragedy has now risen to twelve. So far, none of the bodies retrieved from the burnt-out shell of the building have been identified, but the police are expected to issue a statement later this evening. It is almost certain that the proprietor of the guest house, Mrs Rosemary Feraru (67), and her two full-time staff, Brenda Wickley and Barbara Fry, are among the dead. Attempts to contact Mrs Feraru's son, Michael, have so far proved fruitless. He is understood to be visiting Romania on business . . .

54

EDITED TRANSCRIPT OF TAPE-RECORDED NOTES
MADE BY MIHAI VLĂHUŢA

'I've just realized that it'll be Christmas in two days. There's not much here to celebrate with, but I have to do my best. I'll look outside for a little tree, find some ribbons, and, hey presto, we can all sit round it singing carols. There won't be any turkey, of course, and no plum pudding. Next year, perhaps.'

55

Extract from the Journal of Mihai Vlăhuţa

23 December

Last night, we went to bed around eleven. Liliana had read as much of her grimoire as she could take, and was feeling tired. She asked where Costin was. I told her he had gone to his room, and wanted to be left alone. She had no reason to question me.

For some reason, I felt full of vigour. I could not go to sleep without making love, and, though Liliana was tired, my eagerness roused her. Some might say it was the sight of so much death that filled me with a need for her, but I know it was not that. What I saw in the vault was not death, but everlasting life.

She slept for a while, then woke with a start about three o'clock. I had been awake the whole time. I was too excited to sleep.

'Did you hear something?' she asked.

I had heard nothing. The silence was perfect. Either Costin had stopped banging, too exhausted to go on, or his heart had given out at last.

'There's no whispering,' Liliana said.

'No,' I said. Everything was quiet.

I got out of bed.

'Where are you going?' Liliana asked.

'I want to see how Costin is,' I lied.

'Don't leave me alone.'

'It's all right,' I said. 'I'll only be a moment.'

Before she could stop me, I opened the door and stepped into the corridor. I carried a candle, enough to light my way.

They were all there, as I had known they would be, waiting for me. Matei was ahead of the others, dressed in a sable-lined cloak. He smiled reassuringly at me. There were children among them, as Liliana had said, their eyes wide and eager, their tiny faces pale in the candlelight. Unlike the bodies they had left behind, the *strigoï* were light-skinned and thin. One of them carried a doll, just like the one I had given to Liliana, that was lying beside her at that very moment on the bed.

'It's time,' whispered Matei.

'Yes,' I answered, avoiding those blue, searching eyes. 'It's time. She's inside.'

'Does she know?'

I shook my head. My hand trembled slightly as I pulled back the door and held it open. What I had to do was hard, but it was my duty and my destiny. My ancestry conquered all vulgar emotions. Liliana was a peasant, albeit a peasant with education. The blood of the Vlăhuţas ran in my veins, what possible emotion could conjoin us?

I heard her voice from inside the room, puzzled, a little frightened.

'Mihai, is that you? You've been quick. Is something the matter?'

And then she screamed. A long, piercing scream that echoed along the corridors and rattled the windows and froze the blood. No, perhaps not. They had no blood to freeze, and mine is immune to terror now.

Matei looked at me. He would be the last of them to enter.

'You will not fail me?' he asked.

I shook my head again and gave him a half-smile.

He entered the room and I followed him. They were gathered round the bed in a semi-circle, facing Liliana. She was pressed up against the pillows, cowering, shaking with fear, making a gagging sound deep in her throat.

They parted to let me through. I did not feel the cold, I did not feel, anything but a consciousness of who and what I am. I am not sure if she recognized me. I leaned over her and picked the doll from the pillow. A little girl was standing near me. I handed the doll to her, smiling, and she smiled back.

Matei took her place. He held a knife in his hand, a long Turkish dagger. Its sharp edge caught the light of a candle and twisted it all along its length. Matei stretched his hand out, holding the handle to me. My hand was no longer trembling. I took the dagger from him modestly, with the respect due to one of his age and station. He nodded briefly and stepped back. They were all watching me. I turned back to the bed, to the cowering figure of Liliana. She was naked and shivering, and she could not stop shaking her head from side to side. I smiled at her and shook my head, once to the left and once to the right, and knelt and did my duty while my ancestors watched and sighed with satisfaction.

56

LETTER FROM COUNT MIHAI VLĂHUȚA TO THE RIGHT HONOURABLE SOPHIE WANDLESS

Castel Vlaicu
Satu Vlaicu
Transylvania

25 December

Dear Sophie,

This letter won't reach you till the spring, but I want to write it now, so you will know I was thinking about you at Christmas. You may have gone to Bucharest and been disappointed not to find me there. I'm sorry, but when you hear all that has happened since I last wrote, you will understand. I reached Castel Vlaicu barely in time, before winter set in in earnest, and since then it has been impossible to get messages in or out. As soon as there is a chance, I will have one of the villagers take this letter to the nearest town, where it can be forwarded to you in England. The people in Satu Vlaicu are charming and friendly, and I am sure you will become as fond of them as I have.

They all call me 'Count Mihai', which makes me sound terribly grand, though I assure you I'm far from that. I haven't shaved in weeks, or had a haircut. You'd understand if you could feel how cold it is! Mind you, it does rather make me look like one of the old *boyars* in the portrait gallery at the castle. And I don't mind admitting that being a blue-blooded count is quite gratifying. To tell you the truth, I was always a bit jealous of the fact that your parents were an actual duke and duchess, and not dispossessed refugees from Mitteleuropa.

The castle is wonderful. I've had a little help to knock it into shape, ready for your arrival. We'll have to give the orphanage plan a miss. But I see from family records that we used to own a hunting lodge in a spot that stays open all year round. The deeds go along with those for the castle, so there won't be a problem about ownership. We can provide skiing, shooting, and fishing – and charge a bomb. I have the name of a young Romanian hotelier who's keen as mustard to get the scheme under way. The profits will go towards turning the old family home in Bucharest into an orphanage. You can tell the Arch Druid to keep the donations coming in. And be sure to tell him to send as many of the boys as he can, whole shipments of them if he's able. They'll all be welcome. I'll see they're well looked after.

But none of it would be worthwhile without you. Forget about the job, just hand in your notice and catch the next plane to Bucharest. I'll be here, waiting for you. And, since you ask, yes, I want us to get married. To get married, and have children, and live here happily ever afterwards.

> Eternal love,
> Mihai

PS: Once things are settled, we'll visit England regularly. Now I'm a count and understand such things better, I'd like to see to it that my father and grandfather are fittingly buried.